A Bumpy Ride

"I am perfectly capable of getting to Australia alone."

"I agree. As far as I'm concerned, you could fly your broom over there with no problem at all. However, I saw no point in upsetting your mother by pointing out that fact."

"Of course not. You have to play the Mr. Perfect game for her, don't you? You never let her see that sarcastic part of you."

He grinned. "Me? Sarcastic? Jessica, darling, I'm crushed to hear you could think such a thing. If you didn't want to go with me, all you had to do was speak up and say so."

"And let the family know how much we detest each other?"

Steve's glance slipped smoothly from her face down to her toes, then once again met her furious expression. "I don't detest you, your highness."

Dear Reader:

Welcome to Silhouette Desire—sensual, compelling, believable love stories written by and for today's woman. When you open the pages of a Silhouette Desire, you open yourself up to a whole new world— a world of promising passion and endless love.

Each and every Silhouette Desire is a wonderful love story that is both sensuous *and* emotional. You're with the hero and heroine each and every step of the way—from their first meeting, to their first kiss . . . to their happy ending. You'll experience all the deep joys—and occasional tribulations—of falling in love.

This month, look for *Candlelight for Two* by Annette Broadrick, which is the highly anticipated sequel to *A Loving Spirit*. And don't miss Kathleen Korbel's terrific *Man of the Month*, *Hotshot*. Of course, I think every July Silhouette Desire is a winner!

So enjoy. . .

Lucia Macro
Senior Editor

ANNETTE BROADRICK

CANDLELIGHT FOR TWO

SILHOUETTE *Desire*

Published by Silhouette Books New York

America's Publisher of Contemporary Romance

SILHOUETTE BOOKS
300 East 42nd St., New York, N.Y. 10017

ISBN: 0-373-05577-3

First Silhouette Books printing July 1990

Printed in the U.S.A.

ANNETTE BROADRICK

lives on the shores of The Lake of the Ozarks in Missouri, where she spends her time doing what she loves most—reading and writing romantic fiction. "For twenty-five years I lived in various large cities, working as a legal secretary, a very high-stress occupation. I never thought I was capable of making a career change at this point in my life, but thanks to Silhouette I am now able to write full-time in the peaceful surroundings that have turned my life into a dream come true."

For JoAnn Slead . . .
Who will always be my "bosom buddy!"

One

"What are *you* doing here?''

Jessica Sheldon's demand hung in the soft morning air, her exasperated tone hiding the shock that swept over her when she saw Steven Donovan sitting at the breakfast bar of her mother's kitchen. She had arrived late the night before, under the impression that she would be alone for the next few days in the home owned by Steve's father and her mother. She had looked forward to the solitude and the opportunity to rest after months of following her hectic schedule.

Jessica had purposely arrived early from her apartment in New York City so that she could enjoy the quiet serenity of the lake home located in Missouri during a time when she knew that Sabrina and Michael had taken their six-year-old twins, David and

Diane, to Florida. Michael's son was the last person she had expected to find there.

She had never been comfortable around Steve during the seven years their parents had been married. Consequently, over the years she had managed to avoid being in his company as much as possible. When she'd made her travel plans, she hadn't thought to ask her mother if Steve would be there, since the last she had heard he was working as a television news reporter out of London.

So what was he doing at the Lake of the Ozarks?

Steve slowly lowered the cup of coffee he had just lifted to his mouth and stared at her. His blue-eyed gaze seemed to take in everything about her, not only her tousled appearance, but her thoughts and feelings as well, as though she had been thoroughly searched and no longer had any secrets from him. This particular trait of his was just one of the reasons she avoided him whenever possible.

"Probably for the same reason you're here, princess," he murmured. He nodded toward a pot of coffee sitting on the cabinet. "Pour yourself a cup of coffee and try to contain your joy at finding me here." As he took another sip of coffee, he watched her over the rim of the cup, his riveting blue eyes filled with a mocking light.

Jessica closed her eyes for a moment, trying to hang on to the sense of peace she'd felt as soon as she had awakened. If only she could understand why this man had such a powerful effect on her. She considered herself to be a calm, rational person with remarkable control over her emotions...except where Steve

Donovan was concerned. For reasons she had never been able to understand, as soon as he opened his mouth around her she invariably became agitated, like a flustered schoolgirl being noticed by a boy for the first time. Her reaction irritated her because he seemed to be the only male who affected her that way.

As an editor of a New York-based travel magazine, Jessica came into contact with an assortment of men of all ages and personalities and had learned to deal with them on a professional basis. Her personal life included a variety of men with whom she shared common interests and she could hold her own with them with equanimity. Her childish response to Steve made no sense.

Jessica realized she was standing in the middle of her mother's kitchen taking slow, deep breaths with her eyes closed, no doubt convincing Steve she was a complete idiot. She opened her eyes and moved over to the coffeepot where she poured herself a cup, noticing that the hand holding the pot had a slight tremor.

Get a hold of yourself, she mentally warned herself. *You're a grown woman, a successful, professional woman. You are not a child.*

She turned and gave Steve a rather weak smile, then joined him at the kitchen bar. At least sitting at his side she did not have to look at him. Now they shared the view of the lake.

Jessica tried not to think about what she must look like at the moment. Gone was her neat, professional appearance—her shoulder-length blond hair neatly tucked into a chignon and a dress-for-success suit.

Because she had thought herself to be alone, Jessica had wandered into the kitchen wearing a faded nightshirt left over from her college days, her hair tumbled around her shoulders and her eyes still swollen from sleep.

She tugged at the hemline of her shirt and found it could not be pulled down lower than midthigh and tried to reason with herself. Why was she so self-conscious? The only thing Steve had on at the moment was a pair of cutoff jeans, leaving his broad chest and long muscled legs bare. From the corner of her eye she noted that he had already taken advantage of the sun. His thigh, which was only a few inches from her own, was several shades darker than hers.

Jessica could feel the heat in her face mount when she realized that he had noticed the direction of her eyes. She forced herself to meet his amused gaze.

"Do Mom and Michael know you're here?" she asked, in a tone she hoped revealed only casual interest.

"Of course they know I'm here. I'm not in the habit of dropping in uninvited."

"I talked to Mother a few days ago. She never mentioned that you were here." Jessica made a mental note to discuss with her mother the obvious oversight.

He shrugged. "She probably didn't see the need. There's plenty of room."

So much for casual conversation. Another trait of Steve's that irritated Jessica was his lack of polite conversation. Invariably he was blunt and to the point, sometimes insultingly so.

She didn't know how to deal with him and she knew it.

So what was she going to do now? For years Jessica had assiduously avoided spending time alone with Steve. She had always made sure that someone else was around to carry on a conversation in order not to find herself in a situation such as the one she was in now.

The problem was, she didn't know what to say to the man. They were family but were not related to each other. The only thing they had in common was their love for their respective parent and for the twins.

She knew that he enjoyed David and Diane as much as she did, not only because Sabrina kept her informed on how often he visited and sent them cards and gifts but from the way the twins talked about him whenever she was around. Her mother invariably spoke of him with loving affection.

From everything that her mother had said about him over the years, Jessica was certain that Steve had many sterling qualities. In fact, there were times when she fully expected him to rip open his shirt to reveal the bright red S underneath.

The trouble was, Jessica had never found any burning desire on her part to get to know him better. She was content to think of him as a very distant speck on her own personal horizon and had been quite successful in keeping the necessary distance from him until now.

"I take it you're here on vacation, too?" she finally asked in the deepening silence.

"More or less. I have a new assignment and decided to stop off on the way, since I haven't seen the family in some time." When she didn't say anything more, he added, "I hope my being here hasn't disrupted any plans you might have made."

"Oh, no. Not at all. I haven't made any plans. Not really." She shifted in her chair and once again tugged at the hem of her night shirt.

He smiled, as though aware of her nervousness, and Jessica once again rushed to fill in the silence. "When did you get here?"

"About a week ago. I promised them that I would stay until they return." His grin was mischievous. "I insisted they go, otherwise David and Diane would never have forgiven me for ruining their plans to see Disney World."

"They're supposed to be back tomorrow, aren't they?"

"So they told me."

All right, she told herself. *Accept what you can't change.* She was here now. So was he. Surely she could deal with this unexpected hitch in her vacation plans. She could manage to spend a few hours around him, no matter how uncomfortable she felt. If only she didn't feel as though he knew what she was feeling, giving her the sense of being at a disadvantage. He couldn't read her mind, after all. There was no reason for her to be nervous around him.

Steve got up and poured himself another cup of coffee. "Sabrina tells me that you were recently promoted."

"Yes." She nodded her head and took a nervous sip of coffee without looking at him.

"Still working for that travel magazine?"

She glanced up at him and forced herself to smile. "Yes." She couldn't face his steady regard. She dropped her gaze and studied the liquid in her cup, unable to think of anything else to say.

"A promotion must mean you're enjoying your job."

She nodded without looking at him. "Yes. Yes, I am." She raised her cup to her lips.

"How about going to bed with me?"

Jessica spilled coffee all over the counter, her face flaming. "What!"

He grinned. "I was just making sure you were paying attention. You were being so damned agreeable, I thought I'd check it out."

She hastily wiped up the spilled liquid with a paper towel. "I'm afraid I've never grown accustomed to your sense of humor," she muttered, pouring herself a fresh cup.

Once again silence reigned in the kitchen.

Jessica found the soothing view familiar and infinitely relaxing. The quiet lake atmosphere was a far cry from her hectic existence in Manhattan, but she loved her job and wouldn't consider changing it in order to live anywhere else. She tried to forget about the man leaning on the counter next to her. She had almost succeeded in relaxing when he spoke once more.

"I'm enjoying my job as well, thanks for your interest," he said in a friendly tone. "I've been in the

London news bureau for two years now. The network has given me a couple of nice promotions. I've done some interesting travel and—''

''I know,'' she said. ''Your press agent keeps me fully informed about all of your activities.''

He lifted his brows. ''My who?''

''Your press agent—my mother.''

He laughed. ''No kidding. I didn't know that Sabrina ever mentioned me to you.''

''Oh, yes. She talks about you all the time. She couldn't be any more proud of you than if you were her own son.''

He leaned his forearms on the counter and looked at her. ''Does that bother you?''

She gave a startled laugh. ''Not really. Why do you ask?''

''Oh, I don't know. The two of you were on your own for most of your life, weren't you?''

She nodded. ''Yes. My father was killed when I was two.''

''It would be natural for you to resent her interest in someone else.''

Great. Now she had to deal with an amateur psychologist, as well. ''Only if I were neurotic,'' she responded. ''I was pleased when Mom fell in love with Michael. The twins were an added bonus.''

''I notice you aren't commenting on the joys of suddenly finding yourself with a stepbrother two years older than you.''

Jessica tried to look unruffled. ''I haven't given it much thought.''

''I make you nervous, don't I?''

"This may come as a real shock to you, Steve, but I rarely give you any thought at all." Her exasperation finally won out.

"Don't you? Then why have you gone to so much effort to avoid me?"

"What nonsense. I don't know what you're talking about!"

"Every time I've agreed to come home for some family gathering you've always turned up missing with Sabrina making your last minute excuses."

She pushed her hair back from her face. "I believe that's a slight exaggeration. I've only had to cancel a trip twice in the seven years they've been married."

"Uh-huh. Both times when I was going to be here."

"A coincidence. Nothing more."

His smug smile let her know that he didn't believe her. She would have loved to wipe it off his face but found herself working hard to control her temper. What an exasperating man he was!

"Your mom keeps me up-to-date on your activities, too, you know. Are you still dating that advertising executive?"

She jerked her head around. "Mom told you about Devin?"

"Was that his name? I believe she mentioned him once or twice."

Oh, Mother, how could you? It is none of Steve Donovan's business who I date, or where I work, or what I'm doing with my life!

"I had no idea you would be so interested in my social affairs," she finally said.

He grinned. "Almost as much as the interest you've shown in my career," he admitted.

For the first time since she had entered the room, the look they shared was filled with mutual understanding.

"I think your mom wants us to be friends, princess."

Jessica wished she knew why he insisted on calling her by that ridiculous name. He started it the second or third time they were together; she couldn't remember exactly when that was. All she knew was that she detested the nickname and wished she understood why he used it. However, she was not about to give him the satisfaction of knowing she was curious about it.

"I can't imagine why. Under different circumstances the two of us would never have met." Her temper was gradually getting the best of her. Even she could hear the anger in her voice. How had he managed to put her on the defensive...and keep her there?

His smile was filled with mockery. He knew very well what he was doing. "Perhaps she thought that once we really got to know each other we'd discover the same attraction she and Dad have for each other."

"Hah!"

"Am I supposed to interpret the meaning of that erudite comment?"

She glanced at him. "Would fat chance make the meaning any more clear?" She bared her teeth in a semblance of a smile.

He nodded. "I was close to that interpretation and I must admit that I heartily concur. Why anyone would be attracted to a spoiled, vain, egotistical person like you is more than I—''

"What? Me? Spoiled? Vain? Coming from you, that is really amusing. I have never known anyone who was so convinced of his own superiority as you are. Just because I don't fall on my knees whenever you happen to walk in the door—'' She paused, taking a deep breath. ''And as far as my being egotistical, that really is laughable, coming from you! You are so insufferably arrogant—''

He held up his hand. ''All right. I get the picture. What we have here is a mutual lack of admiration society. There's no reason to debate the particulars. Your opinion of me is similar to mine of you.''

''You are nothing to me. As far as I'm concerned, you don't exist.''

''Well, princess, after seven years we've managed to get it out in the open.'' He held out his hand. ''Congratulations.''

She looked at him, then down at his hand with unconcealed suspicion. ''For what?''

''For being honest for probably the first time in your li'l ol' life,'' he drawled. ''That honey-wouldn't-melt-in-my-mouth attitude of yours has been so phony it curdled my stomach.''

''*Me* a phony? That's a laugh. Just watching you swoop down on the family with all the hugs and flashing smiles was enough to keep me away from family gatherings for years.'' She stopped suddenly, realizing what she had just admitted. Darn. How had he managed to get under her skin so quickly? Where was all her self-control that she took so much pride in?

How had he caused her to admit to feelings that she had never consciously faced before?

A thoughtful moment of silence hung between them before Steve finally said, "Well, at least you're now willing to admit it. That's a start. Who knows? Maybe we'll manage to clear the air between us before the family returns."

She stood and walked over to the sink. "What is there to clear?" she asked, rinsing out her cup.

"We've agreed that we're not going to be charter members of one another's fan club. That's a start, isn't it?"

She turned and leaned against the sink, crossing her arms over her chest. "I suppose." She looked out the window before glancing back at him. "In the meantime, we've got today to get through. What do you suggest we do?"

He cocked his head, as though thinking. "Well, we could avoid each other as much as possible."

"An endeavor that has definite appeal to me, I assure you." At the moment Jessica could think of nothing she'd prefer more than not to have to see Steve's mocking expression for the rest of the day.

"Or, we could pretend that we have nothing against each other and enjoy some of the fun of being here on the lake—take the boat out for a few hours, maybe. Do a little swimming."

The thought of spending the day on the boat alone with Steve made her shiver with distaste, an action he observed and acknowledged with a quirk of his lips.

"And I love you, too, princess."

All right! That did it! She'd had it with his pet name for her. "Stop calling me that!"

"Then stop acting like royalty who has to mingle with us peasants!"

Jessica knew that her face was flushed, a physical condition she couldn't control when she was furious. And boy, was she furious! How could a man as kind, compassionate and loving as Michael Donovan have ever produced a son like Steve?

However, the fact remained that Steve *was* Michael's son and she was a guest in Michael's home. She couldn't abuse his hospitality even when he wasn't there. Whatever her personal opinion, she would have to draw on the manners that her mother had hammered into her while Jessica was growing up.

That was the problem. Jessica never felt grown-up when she was around Steve. She wanted to kick, yell, punch and sock the man, anything to wipe that infuriating know-it-all smirk off his face.

She forced herself to project a calmness she didn't feel. "A boat ride sounds nice. I could use a few hours of relaxing and not having to do anything but soak up some sun." Her eyes met his and she smiled as though he were a new acquaintance.

He lifted his brow. "I wouldn't want you to strain yourself trying to be polite around me, your highness. Are you sure you could handle a day alone with me without attempted homicide?"

She counted to ten before she muttered "Try me!" through gritted teeth.

He slowly came over and set his cup on the counter beside her. "Don't tempt me," he said with a slow smile, his lips almost touching her cheek before he moved away.

Steve turned and walked out of the kitchen, leaving Jessica alone.

Two

Jessica made sure she was close enough to the house to hear the car when the family arrived home the next day. She raced outside and was there to greet the twins when they tumbled out of the car.

David Michael Donovan was twenty-five minutes older than Diane Michelle, a fact that he enjoyed pointing out to his sister on a regular basis. David had his mother's red hair and green eyes, but the irrepressible grin reminded Jessica of Michael...and of Steve. Diane had her father's dark hair and silver-gray eyes and an elfin face.

Jessica loved them both to distraction and had missed them enormously since she had moved to New York. They were as much a part of her as if she had given birth to them.

Both twins fell upon her with shouts and hugs and she found herself kneeling on the pavement of the driveway with her arms wrapped around them, tears unashamedly sliding down her face.

Michael walked around the car and opened Sabrina's door. He kept his arm around her waist as they walked toward the trio beside the car.

"We didn't know you were going to be here when we got home, sissy," Diane exclaimed. "Mommy said she wasn't sure when you'd get here."

David kept saying over and over, "We brought you something from Disney World, sissy. Just wait until you see it. We brought you something!"

Michael grinned at Sabrina. "I would say that our little whirlwinds are glad to see their sister, wouldn't you?"

Sabrina smiled, fully aware of how much she had missed her older daughter. They had always been so close and she missed that now, even though they talked on the phone frequently. She noticed that Jessica had acquired a very becoming tan that enhanced her blond beauty.

Sabrina's two daughters couldn't look more different from each other. Each of them looked more like their fathers. But the love shared by all of them was overwhelmingly obvious.

"Where's Steve?" she asked Jessica when her daughter finally came to her feet and gave her mother a big hug.

"I'm just fine, Mom. It's great to see you, too."

Michael laughed and hugged Jessica to him. "Don't let your mother fool you, honey. She's been so impatient to get home to see you, I thought we were going to have to cut our vacation short. Either that, or fly her home ahead of us.''

Jessica looked around at her mother and found Sabrina blushing. ''Well, I've missed you,'' her mother admitted. ''There's nothing surprising about that, is there?''

''I've missed you, too, Mom. I've missed all of you. I'm so glad you're home.''

''How did you and Steve get along?'' Sabrina asked.

Turning away to help Michael with some of the bags, Jessica searched frantically for a response that would be truthful without being upsetting to Sabrina. Jessica knew very well how much her mother wanted her to like and get along with Steve.

She kept her head turned away as she murmured, ''Oh, Steve and I get along all right. We understand each other.'' She happened to glance up from the trunk at that moment and catch Michael watching her. He winked at her, then turned away and started into the house with some of the luggage.

He knows how I feel about Steve, Jessica realized with a start. A sense of guilt shimmered into her consciousness. *How awful! I wouldn't hurt Michael for the world.* She handed a small bag to each of the twins, grabbed one last piece of luggage and closed the trunk.

''I'm so glad you're here, darling,'' Sabrina said as they walked into the house together. ''We so seldom get the whole family together, especially since Steve has been overseas working. I've been so excited knowing that we would have a few days together as one big happy family.''

Jessica forced a smile.

Steve met them as soon as they got inside. He hugged Sabrina and swung her around in his arms before both twins grabbed him and started clinging.

Jessica watched her mother laughing and talking with Steve and the twins, her enjoyment and delight obvious. Steve's words of the day before suddenly came back to her and for the first time Jessica identified one of the feelings she was experiencing at the moment.

Jealousy.

She had never resented Michael coming into her mother's life and had welcomed the twins, but it was Steve that always caused a reaction in her. The easy way he related to Sabrina caused a definite pang within Jessica. There was a closeness between Steve and Sabrina that Jessica had never understood. Whatever had caused it, she realized that she felt left out of the charmed circle.

The unexpected knowledge shook her with its implications. Her? Jealous of Steve? How ridiculous! How trite! She sighed. How true.

Why hadn't she seen her reactions earlier for what they were? Of course she still found him irritating and arrogant, not to mention egotistical, but she also recognized that she envied him his easy acceptance of the new family that had been formed.

Jessica had always thought she'd accepted the situation . . . until now. She loved the twins. Absolutely adored them. And Michael was everything a husband

and father should be. However, her reaction to Steve should have given her a clue that she had not worked through all the ramifications of the union.

A sense of shame swept over her. How could she be jealous of a man she rarely saw? How embarrassing! She shook her head and turned back into the conversation in time to hear Steve explaining to her mother how they had spent their time together!

"Jessica and I have used the rare opportunity of being together to get better acquainted. We spent yesterday out on the lake, then went out for dinner last night, danced awhile." Couldn't they see the mocking light in his eye when he glanced over at her and smiled?

How could he make their time together sound so congenial when it had been more of an armed truce?

She smiled at her mother. "Oh, yes, I would have to say that our time together has been very educational." She faced Steve's enigmatic look with one of her own. He wasn't the only person who could fake civility.

For the rest of the day she was regaled with stories about Florida and all the sights the twins had seen. They had brought her back various souvenirs for which she was suitably enthusiastic and complimentary regarding their choices.

"I just wish you could have been there with us, sissy," Diane lamented. "Then you wouldn't have had to be here all by yourself and be lonesome for us."

"She wasn't lonesome, dummy," her brother interjected. "Steve was here to keep her company, remember?"

"Don't call me names, David. 'Member what Mama said."

"Then don't act so dumb and I won't have to keep telling ya," he pointed out with six-year-old logic.

"I didn't know if Jessica knew Steve. She's never here when he comes to visit," Diane pointed out.

"Of course she knows him. He's her brother."

Diane looked at Jessica in surprise. "Steve is your brother, too?"

Jessica felt as though she were at a tennis match, her head going back and forth as the twins volleyed their words. She had to pause for a moment to get her bearings before she answered.

"Actually," she said in a carefully neutral voice, "no, he's not."

A complete silence fell upon the room as the twins looked at each other—David with astonishment, Diane with a hint of smugness. Obviously, her brother didn't know *every*thing.

"He's not?" David asked, sounding confused.

"No."

"You're my sister, aren't you?"

"Yes."

"And Steve's my brother, isn't he?"

"Yes."

"Then why isn't he your brother, too?" he demanded to know. From his expression Jessica guessed that David felt adults deliberately tried to be confusing.

"I know it's hard to understand, love, but Steve and I don't have the same mother or father. You and I have the same mother. You and Steve have the same father. Do you understand?''

He stared at her for a moment, his brow furrowed. "I guess so," he said with more than a hint of doubt.

Jessica chuckled. "It's nothing to be concerned about, believe me." She hugged both children to her. "So tell me what else you did on your vacation."

That was all the incentive either child needed to talk nonstop trying to explain everything they had seen and done during the week they were gone in five minutes or less. Jessica settled back to listen with a smile on her face.

Later in the day, Jessica and Sabrina were in the kitchen preparing dinner when Sabrina turned to her daughter with a look of expectancy. "So tell me all about yesterday...where you went, what you did."

Jessica poured two glasses of tea and handed one to her mother. "First, I have a question for you, Mom. Why didn't you tell me that Steve was going to be here when I called to say I was coming?"

Sabrina's expression was the epitome of innocence. "What difference would it have made? You know we have plenty of room for both of you. Besides, I thought this was a perfect chance for the two of you to become better acquainted." She grinned. "And it looks as though it worked. Steve seemed quite pleased about the time you've had together."

Jessica almost groaned. "That's because he knew that was what you wanted to hear. Contrary to what he said, we barely spoke to each other all day."

Sabrina studied Jessica's set expression for a moment before she asked with real curiosity, "Don't you like Steve?"

Jessica sighed and turned away. She removed the casserole from the refrigerator and placed it in the oven, then began to set the table.

"Of course I like Steve, Mom. What's not to like? He's good-looking, charming, successful, dotes on you and the twins, not to mention the fact that he's loyal, brave and true."

Laughter rang from the other room as Michael appeared from downstairs. Jessica was mortified that she hadn't heard his approach before she blurted out her retort. She felt herself flushing with embarrassment. "I'm sorry," she managed to say.

"Don't apologize on my account, Jessica. Even though he's my son and I love him dearly, I, too, get a little weary of hearing Sabrina sing his praises from time to time."

"Michael!" Sabrina stared at her husband in surprise. "You make me sound like a star-struck teenager or something."

He leaned over and kissed her, her lips still moist from the iced tea. "All I'm saying is that I can understand that Jessica might find the subject of Steve a trifle boring."

Jessica flashed him a grateful look and changed the subject and peace reigned in the kitchen.

She waited until they were all gathered around the dinner table, finishing their light dessert, to spring her news on the family.

"I have an announcement to make."

Everyone looked at her expectantly. Oh, this was going to be worth the wait, watching their faces as she shared her exciting news. "I've been assigned to write a comprehensive travel article about Australia, which means that when I leave here, I'll be flying to San Francisco to catch a flight to Sydney."

Her news caused a sudden burst of conversation around the table.

"Australia? Where's that?" David asked.

"Don't they have kangaroos and those cuddly bears there?" Diane added.

"Congratulations, Jessica. That's quite an assignment." This came from Michael.

Sabrina looked delighted. She glanced at Steve with a question in her eyes. Jessica looked at the man who was seated beside her. He had a very strange expression on his face. She turned back to her mother. What was going on?

"But this is wonderful! What a fantastic coincidence!"

"Coincidence?"

"Steve must have told you that he's on his way to Australia for his next assignment. Why, things couldn't have worked out better for you, darling. You and Steve can travel to Australia together!"

Jessica's fork fell out of her hand and clattered onto her plate. She was too rattled to notice the look Steve and Michael shared. "I really don't think our traveling together is necessary, Mom." She glanced at Steve with an unspoken plea for help. "I'm sure your plans are already set up and everything. I wouldn't want to impose—"

"Where are you going?" he asked, ignoring her agitation.

"Sydney, then perhaps on to Melbourne. I have several contacts to make when I first arrive. After talking with them, I'll decide what areas I want to explore for the article."

He shrugged. "I don't see a problem in our traveling together, then. I won't be able to look after you once we arrive, but—"

"I don't need anyone to look after me. I'm perfectly capable of traveling alone." She turned to Sabrina. "Really, Mother. I'm not a child. Just because I've never done any international traveling before doesn't mean I can't manage on my own."

"I never thought you couldn't, darling," Sabrina responded, a puzzled frown on her face. "It was just a suggestion, after all."

"I think it's a good one, Sabrina," Steve offered with a smile. "After all, what's the point of having a big brother if you don't take advantage of the relationship once in a while? I'll be glad to look after her."

A trio of voices answered him as the twins and Jessica all said, "She's not—" "I'm not—"

"—your sister."

The other three looked surprised at the choral effort. Steve was the first to recover. "Of course I know that you aren't *really* my sister, but you're definitely family." He met her gaze with a steady one of his own. "Unless, of course, you would prefer not to be associated with me in any way." Once again his gaze met his father's questioning glance.

What could she say? Short of being inexcusably rude, how could she turn down a polite offer to escort her to Australia? The infuriating thing about his offer was that she knew he didn't want her along any more than she wanted to be there. So why hadn't he made some excuse? Why make her look like the churlish one?

She gave what she hoped was a nonchalant shrug. "It's all right with me if Steve doesn't mind." She refused to look at him.

"Oh, good," Sabrina responded. "I know you'll enjoy yourself so much more with someone along who's used to traveling."

"How long are you supposed to be over there, Jessica?" Michael asked.

"No more than two weeks. If I get my article blocked out before then, I'll come back early." She turned to Steve. "What are your plans?"

"I'm doing some research and background investigation on a possible story. I've also accumulated some vacation time that I intend to take while I'm over there."

"I see."

Steve knew that she didn't see because he was purposely misleading her. Because of his father's background in law enforcement, Steve had told Michael the truth—researching a story was part of his cover for being there. Michael was the only one in the family who knew that Steve worked for the United States government first, the television network second.

Not even Michael was aware, though, of the seriousness of what he was trying to find out.

Steve knew that he should have refused to allow Jessica to travel with him but he couldn't resist the opportunity to watch her squirm. She was such a little hypocrite, pretending that the two of them got along. He'd wondered how she would get herself out of this one. Obviously she had decided not to try, so he was stuck with her, at least until they reached Sydney.

After their arrival he'd disappear and let her play tourist over there while he got on with the job assigned to him.

Steve lifted his glass and gave a mocking toast. "Well, mate," he said in his best Aussie accent, "looks like you've got yourself an offsider for the next few days."

Everyone laughed, everyone but Jessica. She took a sip of her drink, then began to ask questions of the twins, knowing the subject of Australia would not be brought up again at the table. What she had to say to Steve was better said in private.

She waited patiently for the family to disburse after dinner. Eventually the twins went to bed and Sabrina and Michael disappeared into their room. Steve had gone outside on the deck as soon as dinner was over. Once everyone else left, Jessica followed him outside.

"We need to talk," she said, closing the sliding door behind her.

Steve stood by the railing, his forearms resting on its broad width. Without bothering to glance around he said, "Somehow that doesn't surprise me. What's bothering you now, your highness?"

"You know exactly what's bothering me. Why did you agree to travel with me to Australia? You're fully aware of my feelings on the subject of being around you."

Steve lazily turned his head until he made eye contact. "We haven't entered into a marriage contract, you know. All I agreed to do was to see that you made it across the Pacific without ending up in Europe somewhere."

"I do not need your help, or anyone else's, for that matter. I am perfectly capable of getting to Australia alone."

"I agree. As far as I'm concerned, you could fly your broom over there with no problem at all. However, I saw no point in upsetting Sabrina by pointing out that fact."

"Of course not. You have to play the Mr. Perfect game for her, don't you? You never let her see that sarcastic part of you."

He grinned. "Me? Sarcastic? Jessica, darling, I'm crushed to hear you could think such a thing." He straightened, turning so that they stood only a few inches apart. "If you didn't want to go with me, all you had to do was to speak up and say so."

"And let the family know how much we detest each other? That would certainly help family harmony, wouldn't it?"

Steve's glance slid smoothly from her face, down to her toes, then once again met her furious expression. "I don't detest you, your highness. 'Detest' is an emotion-filled word. I'm afraid I can't manage to work up that much feeling about you, one way or the other.''

Jessica had never considered herself to be a passionate person. Therefore, she was more than a little surprised to discover that had she held a lethal instrument in her hand at that moment, she might have come close to attacking the man standing before her.

Steve saw that his last remark had found its mark. Jessica stood there in front of him, so close he could feel her trembling. He was ashamed of himself. Why did he continue to bait her when he really didn't dislike her at all? Granted, he was human enough to resent the fact that she obviously didn't like him, but he'd never been one to care about winning a popularity contest. So why did her obvious animosity toward him manage to get under his skin?

"Look," he said, running his hand through his hair, "I'm sorry. That was uncalled for. I guess I just resent the fact that nothing I can say or do around you seems to make a difference. I need to accept the fact that you don't like me, and just let it go at that." The moonlight cast shadows across her face, but he was able to see the surprise in her expression. He grinned. "Yeah, that must be a first for me. I'm not used to apologizing."

He turned away. "As long as I'm being so damned honest, I might as well tell you something I discovered about myself today. Something that I'm really ashamed of having to admit."

"What is that?" Her tone was wary, which didn't surprise Steve at all.

"I watched you today when you rushed out to the car to greet the family. I saw the twins engulf you and Dad and Sabrina eagerly hug you and I wanted you to greet me like that. I wanted to be a part of that family feeling of warmth and tenderness." He shoved his hands in his pockets. "I'm not proud of the fact that I've been behaving rather badly toward you for no other reason than you don't like me. I really can't blame you for not wanting to travel with me."

Jessica couldn't believe what she was hearing. The great Steve Donovan admitting that he was hurt because she didn't like him? The irony of the situation struck her and she couldn't resist telling him.

"That is really amusing under the circumstances, Steve. I discovered just today that the biggest reason I didn't like you is because I've always been jealous of you!"

He stared at her in shock. "Jealous? Of me?"

"It sounds silly, I know, but it's the truth. You pointed my thinking in that direction with your comments yesterday. I've never been jealous of Michael, or even the twins, but every time I've wanted to share my accomplishments with Mom in the past several years, she would invariably tell me the latest about you—a promotion, a late-breaking story that you covered, a new assignment." Jessica was amazed to discover how much lighter she felt now that she had admitted her feelings to him. "I'd never faced before how childish my attitudes were."

He studied her face in the moonlight. "Well, what do you know?" he finally murmured. He placed his hands on her shoulders. "I would have never guessed.

You've always appeared so self-assured, so regal, so much in control. I had no idea.''

"Try not to let it go to your head," she remarked wryly.

Steve laughed unrestrainedly. Somehow he also managed to pull her into his arms at the same time.

Jessica stiffened. She had never been so close to Steve before and his proximity was having a strong effect on her. She put her hands on his chest in order to provide some necessary breathing space.

Instead of taking the hint, Steve managed to confuse her even more.

He kissed her.

Three

———

Steve glanced at the woman asleep next to him on the plane, then determinedly leaned back in his chair and closed his eyes. He must have lost his mind. He was somewhere over the Pacific Ocean heading toward an assignment and had volunteered to play escort to Jessica Sheldon.

He ought to have his head examined.

He could hear himself now, explaining to the psychiatrist who was always available to any of the men who needed to talk to relieve some of their job-related stress.

"I've got a problem. You see, seven years ago my father married Sabrina Sheldon, a woman infinitely suited for him. I was delighted to be asked to attend the small wedding as his best man."

"When I arrived I was introduced to Jessica Sheldon, Sabrina's daughter. My reaction to her was instant and absolute. She affected me like no other woman ever has, much to my dismay. You have to understand that, even then, my plans were already in motion. I knew what I wanted to do with my life and how I intended to accomplish my goals. Falling for an attractive, aloof woman didn't figure into any of my plans."

"Over the years I've done my best to forget her. Unfortunately, she's managed to make every other woman I meet pale in comparison. I knew I was in big trouble when I saw her again because my reaction was as strong as ever."

"I knew she didn't like me but hadn't a clue why until our last visit. When she finally admitted her reasons, as much as admitting that she knew they weren't valid, the relief I felt was tremendous. You have no idea."

"That's when I made the biggest mistake I've made so far...I kissed her. None of my fantasies could compare with what the reality revealed to me."

"It scared the hell out of me, let me tell you. That kiss ignited a spark that I thought would send us both up in flames."

Steve almost groaned aloud at the memory. He opened his eyes and looked around the darkened cabin, trying to get a grip on his feelings. He noticed that the blanket Jessica had tucked around her shoulders had fallen. Without thinking about it he reached over and carefully covered her once again, his hand lingering on her shoulder.

He would never forget the look of shocked surprise on her face when he'd finally forced himself to end the kiss. Or the way she practically ran to get away from him. At the time he had decided her reaction would serve his purpose as well as any. He should never have allowed himself to be goaded into agreeing to accompany her. Now she would announce to the family that she refused his offer.

Only she hadn't. Jessica had made sure they were never alone again, though. Once they were on the plane to San Francisco it was too late.

His boss wouldn't be pleased if he knew, but Steve didn't intend for Max to find out. As soon as they arrived Steve would escort Jessica to the hotel where she would be staying, then he'd meet his contact as arranged.

He reviewed what he already knew about the case he was investigating.

Five years ago another scandal had broken out with regard to the British intelligence service. Suspicion of a mole in the organization had created a furor. In the midst of all the scandal, Trevor Randall, second in command, had disappeared. No one could make any connections to him and the possibility of a double agent, but his disappearance at that particular time seemed to be more than mere coincidence. His guilt or innocence became a moot point when he was later reported dead in a cottage fire.

Eventually two other men were arrested and tried as traitors to the government and the scandal eventually became yesterday's news.

A few weeks ago, while investigating another story, Steve came across a piece of information that he immediately reported to Max. He'd been given a hint that Trevor Randall may not have died. Before he turned that particular piece of information over to his news media boss, he wanted to know if Max felt the intelligence community would prefer to follow up the lead in secret.

At that time Max admitted to Steve that one of his contacts in the British intelligence office had never bought the story of Trevor's death and had been attempting to follow up with a private investigation when he'd disappeared. Max had never been able to find out anything more. The British government had chosen not to divulge what might have happened to the American who had inquired.

Steve's tip proved to be irresistible to Max. He wanted him to follow up, but to be careful not to make waves. Steve's investigation would have to remain unofficial. If he turned up anything, he could claim his investigative reporting instincts had caused him to follow up on the lead.

However, Max had reminded him of the other agent's disappearance. Steve knew that what he was getting into could be very dangerous.

When he discovered that there was a possibility Trevor Randall had moved to Australia with a new name and identity, Steve convinced Max that he could use the time to check out the story, as well as enjoy a much needed vacation. Max had reluctantly agreed.

There had been no mention of being accompanied by the woman beside him.

Steve shifted in his chair, trying to get comfortable. Glancing at his watch he calculated another eight hours before they would land in Sydney. He had to get some sleep. He forced his thoughts to center on the need for sleep and eventually he found what he was seeking.

The first clue Steve had that his plans were not working out quite as he had imagined came shortly after they cleared customs. They had landed at six-thirty in the morning, Sydney time, and cleared customs with no problem. He intended to rent a car at the airport to take them into town and to Jessica's hotel, when two men suddenly seemed to materialize on either side of him.

"Mr. Donovan?" one of them asked.

Steve held a suitcase in each hand. He immediately set them down and looked around for Jessica. She was a few steps behind him, surveying the airport with a smile of anticipation on her face, obviously pleased to have reached their destination.

So was he, but he hadn't expected a welcoming committee.

"Yes."

"Your car is waiting just outside the terminal. If you'll come this way." The man who spoke had the height and build of a bodyguard. His friend could have been his twin brother.

"There must be some mistake. I haven't ordered a car," he began.

The silent man scooped up both pieces of luggage as though they were empty and strode to the exit. Only then did Jessica notice what was happening.

"Wait a minute. That's my suitcase," she said, starting after the man.

Whatever was happening, Steve couldn't afford to lose sight of Jessica. He grabbed her arm in a similar grip to the one on his arm.

"Hold on."

She spun around. "But that man—"

"I know. It's okay."

Not that he believed anything of the sort but he had to say something. He couldn't let her out of his sight and from the hold the other man had on him, he wasn't going anywhere...not unless he wanted to create a scene.

"What's going on?" Jessica demanded to know.

Good question. Steve turned to the man who was rapidly guiding them through the door. "Perhaps you'd like to explain."

By this time they were outside and Steve saw their luggage disappearing into the back of a white limousine. Obviously whoever was kidnapping them was not destitute. Steve wished that he found the thought more reassuring.

Their escort opened the rear door and motioned for Jessica to get in. She looked at Steve and he nodded. As soon as she settled inside, Steve got in beside her. The door closed behind him and he watched as both men sat in the front seat. Within minutes they were moving smoothly through the airport traffic.

"Could you explain to us what's going on?" Steve asked.

The man in the passenger seat up front glanced around. "Mr. Johanson told us to pick you up from the airport and deliver you to him."

Steve noticed that Jessica started to say something. He took her hand and gently squeezed a warning. "Who is Mr. Johanson?" he asked.

"Our boss."

I knew that, you idiot, Steve thought, but decided it would be more politic to keep his thoughts to himself. "Why would Mr. Johanson feel the need to provide us with transportation?"

All he got was a shrug.

Jessica leaned over and whispered, "What's going on?"

His reply was just as quiet. "I wish I knew."

"You didn't know you were going to be met?"

"As far as I know, no one knew I was coming." He patted her hand. "Don't worry about it. It's obviously a mistake that can be explained away once we arrive."

Jessica studied the man beside her, suddenly wishing that she knew him better. What a time to decide that she could have made better use of her time in the past if she hadn't worked so hard to avoid the man.

She couldn't tell what he was thinking or feeling. He appeared to be relaxed and at ease, as though being accosted by strangers in an airport and whisked away to some undisclosed destination was a common occurrence for him.

Perhaps it was. All she knew was that she was uncomfortable with the idea of spending additional time with him. She had fully expected to see the last of Steve as soon as she arrived at the hotel.

If Jessica had learned only one thing in the past several days, that fact was indelibly etched in her mind—the man beside her was a definite hazard to her peace of mind. She had discovered, much to her disgust, that she was not immune to his charm. His confession of being hurt by her attitude toward him had disarmed her.

However, it was his kiss that had proved to her how very dangerous he could be. Since that night she had kept her distance. So what was she going to do about this latest development?

Jessica glanced out the window. She'd had no idea Sydney was so large. They were moving with a steady flow of traffic. Here she was, at last. She found it difficult to take in everything at once.

"Where does Mr. Johanson live?" Steve asked.

"In the Blue Mountains. We should be there in a couple of hours."

"Now, wait a minute. We don't have time for a side trip. Jessica has appointments for this afternoon and I—"

"We're just following orders."

"But—" Jessica started to say but paused when Steve took her hand once again.

"It won't do any good to argue, princess. We'll have to wait until we can talk with Mr. Johanson."

"But who is he?"

"I have no idea."

"Or why he'd be having us brought to him?"

"No."

"I don't like this."

"I'm not particularly pleased with the developments, myself."

"I was looking forward to a hot shower and a chance to stretch out on a bed for a few hours. I felt like a human pretzel when I woke up this morning."

Steve grinned. He had never seen this side of Jessica before. Her attitude surprised him, but he was pleased she was taking the situation in stride. She wasn't easily rattled.

Of course she had no way of knowing that Johanson could be aware of why Steve had come to Australia. Steve knew that he had no intention of explaining his cover assignment to her. Hopefully whatever was going on could be cleared up shortly after their arrival.

"You could sleep now if you wish," he offered, putting his arm around her and pulling her against his chest. He felt her stiffen for a moment, then relax against him.

"Thanks," was her muffled response.

Once again he had Jessica Sheldon in his arms. He could become addicted to the condition if he weren't careful. Since there was nothing else for him to do at the moment, Steve closed his eyes, as well.

When Steve saw the home where they were brought he acknowledged that whoever Johanson was, he did not suffer from a shortage of funds. They had driven through a wrought iron gate that closed behind them, then followed a winding paved road for a fair distance before pulling up in front of a three-story home.

Steve and Jessica stepped out of the car and followed the man who had done all of the talking since he'd accosted them at the airport. They were shown into a formal drawing room and asked to wait.

"Where does he think we'll go?" Jessica asked, looking around the room.

"I believe he was keeping up the semblance of polite behavior."

"I wouldn't term his behavior in quite those words, myself." She walked over to a large painting and studied it.

"You don't seem particularly frightened," he said, watching her.

She looked around at him, surprised. "Is there some reason why I should be?"

"Not that I'm aware of, but then, I haven't a clue as to what's going on."

She grinned. "I can't believe it. The illustrious Mr. Donovan at a loss. I'll have to write this episode up. Otherwise, no one would believe me."

He walked over to her. "Still baiting me, I see."

She had the grace to blush. "I'm sorry. I'm afraid it's a habit more than anything."

The sound of a door opening caused them both to turn and watch as a tall, slightly stooped man with thinning white hair walked through the door. He paused when he saw the two of them.

"Steven Donovan?" he asked.

"That's correct."

"I'm Eric Johanson. I wasn't aware that you were traveling with someone."

"Had I known of your interest, Mr. Johanson, I would have remedied the oversight."

Johanson nodded, taking the comment at surface value. "You must introduce me."

Steve wanted to debate the point but decided not to push his luck for the time being. "This is Jessica Sheldon. She's an editor for a travel magazine based in New York City. We're old friends. When I heard that she was coming to Australia, I decided to take some of my accrued vacation time and spend it with her." The loving look he gave her caused Jessica's eyes to widen.

"I see. Then you aren't here in your official capacity?"

Steve contrived to look amused. "A man has to play sometime, you know. Why do you ask?"

Johanson was no fool. His gaze took in both of them for a long, studied moment before he said, "Your reputation precedes you, Mr. Donovan. You've made quite a name for yourself in Great Britain with some of your news reporting."

"How did you know I was coming?"

Johanson shrugged. "From your visa application."

A confidential document that most people would not have access to. Interesting, Steve thought.

"Do you meet many planes in a similar fashion, Mr. Johanson?"

"No. You're an exception."

Steve glanced around at Jessica, then deliberately placed his arm around her. "As you can see, my visit is planned for strictly pleasure." When he felt Jessica stiffen, Steve tightened his hold in warning. He glanced at his watch. "I'm afraid we need to be returning to Sydney. I'm sorry if you were hoping for an interview or something of that nature, but—"

"You will be spending the night here, Mr. Donovan," Johanson said quietly.

Steve didn't take his eyes off the older man, even when he felt the jolt that went through Jessica's body at Johanson's words.

"Why?"

"Let's just say that I insist on offering you our hospitality."

"But I've already made appointments for the afternoon," Jessica said, glancing from one man to the other.

Johanson nodded. "I'll show you to your room. There's a phone there where you can call and cancel your afternoon plans." He turned away and opened the door behind him.

Jessica glanced at Steve. What was going on? The undercurrent was too intense to be a product of her imagination. Steve nudged her to follow Johanson out into the hall and up the wide, curving staircase to the second level. He followed, his hand resting lightly against the small of her back.

Johanson paused at the end of the hallway and opened double doors. Jessica almost gasped at the size and the opulent furnishings of the massive bedroom. She looked at Steve uncertainly.

"I believe that you will find everything to your satisfaction," Johanson said, walking over to a door and opening it, revealing a bathroom of gleaming marble and ornate fixtures.

"I take it you and your companion would prefer to share a room."

Steve heard Jessica catch her breath and quickly replied, "Yes, of course. Thank you for your understanding of the situation."

Johanson glanced at his watch. "I'm sure you must be hungry. We'll be serving luncheon within the hour. I'll be waiting for you in the drawing room." With that, their host left them.

Steve finally turned and looked at Jessica, wincing at her expression. "I can explain." he began.

"You can't imagine how relieved I am to hear you say that," she said sweetly.

"Let me rephrase that. I can explain why I think it would be a good idea for us to stay together. I don't know why Johanson is insisting we stay here."

Jessica crossed her arms. "Any explanation would be helpful at this point."

"For the very reason that I don't know why Johanson wants me here convinces me I want to make sure you're all right."

"Why? Do you think he's doing illegal experiments on hapless tourists?" She took a couple of steps away from him, then spun around to face him. "You told me that you were following up on an assignment here. So what is all this nonsense about being here on vacation with me?"

He ran his hand through his hair. "It was the first thing I could come up with, on the spur of the moment. Who knows? Johanson may be a publicity happy fellow who hoped to dazzle us with his wealth in exchange for a mention on national television."

"Is that what you believe?"

He started to answer her, then thought better of it. He turned away and walked over to one of the windows. "No," he finally said without turning to look at her.

She followed him to the window. "Then what's going on?"

"It's obvious that he's suspicious of me. Somehow he may have heard rumors about an investigation I've been working on."

"What kind of investigation?"

"I've been following leads to find out whether a man who supposedly died five years ago is now living under an assumed name somewhere in Australia."

"Why are you looking for him?"

"Because if my theory is right, the man faked his own death rather than be convicted as a spy."

"My God, Steve! You could get yourself killed poking around asking questions about something like that."

"Ah, princess, I didn't know you cared."

She glared at him for a moment, then turned away just as there was a knock at the door. Steve strode across the room and opened the door. Their luggage had arrived.

As soon as they were alone again, Steve motioned to the phone beside the bed. "You had better make your phone calls."

"But what am I going to tell them? That I'm being held captive by a man who's afraid my traveling companion can't be allowed loose in this country?"

Since that was exactly what Steve was afraid was happening, he wasn't too pleased that Jessica had so quickly identified the probable cause of their command appearance.

"No. Just explain that something has come up and that you will get in touch with them later."

She stood there watching him, as though waiting for further explanation. When none came she shook her head and walked over to the phone.

"I don't care what this is all about, Steven Donovan. I have no intention of sharing a bed with you. So you had better come up with a good story for our host before bedtime."

Steve could not resist teasing her. He allowed his gaze to slowly move upward over her body, from her toes to her eyes and watched the color deepen in her face.

"You shouldn't be so quick to turn down such an opportunity, your highness. You might find you wouldn't mind the experience at all."

Four

Jessica found the food delicious, but she had trouble hiding her nervousness. For some reason she found it important not to let either man know how unsettled and uncomfortable she felt.

On the one hand, she was experiencing a definite uneasiness with regard to Steve and why he was in Australia in the first place. What he was doing was dangerous, didn't he understand that? What would he have done if she hadn't happened to be there at the time he was met at the airport? Would he have had more difficulty convincing Mr. Johanson of his vacation plans if he'd been alone?

She wasn't at all sure that Steve would have fared as well. What disturbed her was that she cared. Even though her opinion of him hadn't basically changed—he was still irritating and arrogant—she had to admit that he also had some very appealing qualities, as well. He was honest and forthright. There was no question of his integrity, and she had also noticed that he spoke his pet names for her in a tone that almost made them sound as if they were an endearment.

Which brought her to the second reason she felt so ill at ease. If they were going to continue their stay there, then she had to face up to the very real possibility that she would be sharing a bed with Steve that night.

Jessica wasn't at all sure she was ready for that one. Not that she expected him to take advantage of the forced intimacy. No, he'd made his feelings on that subject very clear. The only reason they were together was because of his affection for her mother and the fact that he could rarely, if ever, turn Sabrina down, regardless of the request.

She wondered what Sabrina would think if she knew what was going on at the moment. Jessica preferred not to speculate on her mother's conclusions and determinedly tuned into the conversation.

"How long have you been a reporter, Mr. Donovan?" Johanson asked.

"Almost five years."

"Do you enjoy prying into other people's business?"

"If what they are doing proves to be newsworthy, yes, I suppose I do."

"Even if they wish to be left alone?"

"I take it you are not particularly interested in being a source of news, are you?" Steve asked his host.

"I've never seen a reason to have private information made public for the sake of titillating bored people's penchant for gossip."

Jessica dropped her head to cover a smile. Steve wasn't exactly having it his own way. When she glanced up she found Steve looking at her with a quizzical expression on his face. She gave him a radiant smile.

He blinked, then returned his attention to his host. "You were saying?" he asked, as though he'd lost the train of conversation.

Johanson looked at Steve, then at Jessica. "How long have you known each other?"

Steve smiled. "I met Jessica seven years ago. It was love at first sight."

Jessica almost choked on her glass of water. He was going to be the death of her yet!

"Seven years? And yet you've made no attempt to formalize the relationship."

Steve shrugged. "We have plenty of time. We were both in college back then. She had her plans for a career. I had mine. There was so much we wanted to accomplish before we both settled down." He smiled at Jessica. "Isn't that right, darling?"

"How can I do anything but agree with you?" she responded, wishing he was close enough to kick under the table. He knew he had her at a definite disadvantage and was enjoying himself enormously.

"Aren't you ready to start a family, Miss Sheldon?" Johanson asked.

Jessica could not believe she was hearing this conversation. What could she say that wouldn't make Steve look like the liar that he was at the moment?

"We've talked about a family, of course," Steve said, gazing at Jessica with a loving expression, "but she insisted that she wanted to get her career going first." He looked at Johanson. "You know how women are these days."

His patronizing tone made Jessica's blood boil. She had no way of knowing if his remarks were part of their act or whether he actually felt that women only had a few uses, bearing children being one of them. Just wait until she got him alone.

"This is my first trip to Australia," Steve went on. "Where would you suggest we visit while we're here? Jessica wants to promote the tourist trade between our two countries. I'm sure she'd benefit from your knowledge."

He was convincing, she had to give him that. He came across as an indolent, not-too-bright playboy who was willingly tagging along behind her, content to keep her bed warm and enjoy the sights.

Jessica didn't understand why she knew his attitude was all a pose, but she did. Perhaps all the years of hearing about Steve Donovan had given her more of an insight into his character than she had first supposed.

He was doing everything possible to lull Mr. Johanson into thinking he was harmless. The question was: was it working?

The rest of the meal was punctuated with stories of various places they might wish to visit. Jessica quickly removed a pad and pen from her purse and took notes, relieved to know that whoever this man was, he didn't intend to keep them captive for long.

Later that evening she no longer felt quite so sanguine. She came out of the bathroom to find Steve already in bed.

Jessica had looked through her belongings more than once, trying to decide what to wear to sleep in that night. Unfortunately, when she had packed she hadn't based her sleep apparel choices on the possibility of sharing a bed with anyone—especially not Steve Donovan.

Her concerns were not alleviated when she saw the covers lying across Steve's waist revealing his bare chest.

"Don't you have something to sleep in?" she asked, trying to sound brusque and unconcerned. Unfortunately, her voice broke midway through her question and ended on a definitely wobbly note.

"I'm wearing them."

She eyed him uncertainly.

"Do you want me to show you?" he asked innocently, reaching for the covers.

"No! I mean, I'll take your word for it."

She walked around the bed and gingerly lifted the covers.

"Do you intend to sleep in your bathrobe?" he asked with amusement.

"Of course not!" But of course she had, right up until the time he'd asked. She quickly untied the sash and slipped her arms out of the sleeves. Tossing the robe toward the end of the bed, Jessica dived for the covers.

"That's quite a seductive gown you're wearing, lady. Flannel, isn't it? Long sleeved, high necked. Obviously you intended to seduce every Australian male who caught your fancy with that getup."

She tucked the covers around her shoulders before turning her head on the pillow to glare at him. He'd turned on his side and was propped up on his elbow, watching her.

"For your information, I packed knowing that it would be winter in Australia. I didn't want to get cold."

He grinned. "Obviously there's no danger of that."

"Would you please turn off the light?" She wasn't about to lean over him in order to reach the lamp on his side of the bed.

Steve obligingly turned and flicked off the light, plunging the room into blessed darkness. At least, that's the way Jessica viewed it. She no longer had to look at Steve, either his dancing eyes, his silly grin, or the broad expanse of chest that he continued to leave uncovered.

Since she had used his chest for a pillow on the way to Mr. Johanson's home, she knew exactly how it felt. She shifted restlessly on the bed, making sure that she was as far on her side as she could go.

"If you don't watch it," he said in a silky voice only inches from her ear, "you're going to fall off the bed."

Her startled movement almost proved his prophecy correct. Jessica caught herself in time, hastily moving more to the center of the bed . . . until she was stopped abruptly by Steve's chest.

"Would you get over!" she demanded. "You don't need to take your half in the middle!"

Thank God he couldn't see her face. She knew it was flaming. His chest wasn't the only part of his anatomy she had touched. Her leg had come into contact with one of his. She wasn't sure how her gown had managed to crawl up her legs, leaving them as bare as his.

The only thing he could possibly be wearing was his underwear. Why had she hoped he'd have the decency to at least wear the bottoms of a pair of pajamas? He probably didn't even own a pair!

"There. Is that better?"

His voice sounded a little farther away and she took a deep breath, forcing herself to relax. "Yes. Thank you."

"You're welcome," he replied, mimicking her prim tone of voice.

Let him make fun of her, she didn't care. All she wanted to do was to get this night over with. Never would Jessica greet the morning sun with more enthusiasm than she would its next appearance.

As soon as she returned to Sydney she would make it clear to Steve that she certainly didn't need him around to look after her. She would have been much better off if she had come to Australia alone.

Jessica closed her eyes and concentrated on her breathing. Inhale two, three, four, exhale two, three, fo—"What are you doing!"

"Oh, for God sake, Jessica. I'm turning over. I don't know how to break the news to you, but I am not after your delicious, delectable body. I happen to sleep better on my stomach and therefore I was preparing myself for sleep. Does that meet with your approval, your highness?"

This time his tone held no hint of endearment.

She refused to answer him. Of course she knew he wasn't going to try anything with her. Why should he? He probably had so many women chasing him that he'd had to travel halfway around the world to get away from them. That's probably the real reason why he needed a vacation!

Jessica suddenly had a vision of Steve racing along a beach with a horde of screaming women chasing him in various states of undress.

She giggled, then hastily covered her mouth.

Once again she felt the bed move. "Now what," he said in a voice fraught with impatience.

"Nothing."

"Look, Jessica, there's nothing to get upset about. I'm sorry I got you involved with this. Accompanying you to Australia was not one of my better ideas, I admit it. But there's no reason to cry."

"I'm not crying."

"Oh."

"I was laughing."

The bed shifted suddenly, slanting the mattress so that she slid a few inches toward the center. The length of his body stopped her.

"Laughing! Don't tell me you're going to get hysterical on me."

She couldn't help it. She suddenly found his disgusted tone of voice irresistibly amusing. "No, I'm not." Unfortunately the words were interspersed with more chuckles, as though she in fact was losing control of her emotions. She found herself trying to explain before she realized what she was saying. "I just had this ridiculous picture of you running for your life from all these women chasing after you, wanting your body." She ended her recital with a peal of laughter.

"And exactly what do you find so damned amusing about the idea?"

His wounded vanity caused her to lose the slight control she had over her giggles. "Nothing. I'm sure it's every man's fantasy of how he'd like to go... mobbed by a bunch of beauties wanting to love him." Another peal of laughter caught her off guard.

Steve reached for her in the dark. Unfortunately his aim was a little off. Instead of her arm his hand touched her breast, then quickly moved to her shoulder.

"Damn it, Jessica, stop it! I know you're tired and scared, but there's no reason to lose control."

She tried to tell him she was all right, but he refused to listen to her. The next thing she knew he'd jerked her to him, his mouth covering hers.

As an antidote to hysteria, Jessica decided, she much preferred the kiss to a slap. However, she wasn't hysterical and she hadn't needed a reminder of how she responded whenever Steve kissed her.

But it was too late.

As soon as his lips touched hers, Steve was aware that she froze, but he didn't care. He pulled her closer, wrapping his arms and legs around her and holding her close. She had every reason to be scared. She'd held up very well, considering the circumstances.

All he wanted to do was to reassure her, let her know that he was there, ready to protect her from harm. When she relaxed against him he no longer thought about anything but the fact that he held Jessica in his arms.

She felt wonderful pressed against him. Her gown was somewhere around her thighs. He rubbed his leg against the soft silkiness of hers, enjoying the friction caused by the hair on the calf and thigh of his leg sliding against the smoothness of hers.

He forgot the purpose of the kiss, forgot everything but enjoying the slight floral scent of her, the taste of her, the intoxicating feel of her. He pulled back slightly, not enough to lose contact with her mouth—only enough to place his hand between them. He rested it at the base of her throat, feeling the steady pounding of her pulse against his fingertips.

Then he had to breathe.

Steve raised his head, gasping for air, and heard Jessica's soft panting sigh as she quickly drew breath. The faint noise had never sounded more seductive to him.

Once again his mouth sought hers. This time he allowed his hand to slowly wander, touching the lace at her throat, finding the row of buttons that marched primly down across her chest. As though it had a mind of its own, his hand quickly unfastened three of the buttons, then insinuated itself beneath the folds of flannel, finding the bare softness of her skin.

This was Jessica, the woman who had haunted his dreams for years, the woman he'd tried to forget with other women.

Steve slipped his thigh between hers and gently pressed against her.

Jessica knew that if she didn't stop what was happening, *right now*, she would not have the strength to deny him the inevitable conclusion.

She forced herself to pull away from him, pushing against his chest with trembling hands. "No, Steve. We can't!"

The abrupt sound of her voice in the quiet room caught Steve's attention and he became aware of what he was doing. He jerked away from Jessica as though she had burned him, which was a fairly accurate description of what he was feeling. Only he felt as though he were still on fire.

He jerked the covers away and sprang out of bed. Once inside the bathroom, he closed the door, flipping on the light at the same time. Without looking into the mirror Steve reached in and turned on the water in the shower. He shucked off his briefs and stepped under the cold water, which felt like melted icicles to his overheated body.

Damn, damn, damn. What in hell did he think he was doing, anyway?

It was one thing to indulge in harmless fantasies. It was another thing to decide to live them. He took the punishment of the water for several minutes before finally stepping out and drying off. He pulled on his briefs once more, turned out the light and opened the door to the darkened bedroom. He waited for his eyes to adjust before he carefully made his way to the bed.

Without saying a word Steve crawled into bed making sure he gave Jessica plenty of space. He lay on his side away from her, trying to forget she was there, trying to forget what had almost happened, what he had wanted to happen.

"Steve?"

"Go to sleep."

"I'm sorry."

"Go to sleep."

"I'm not blaming you for what happened."

"Go to sleep."

"We both just got carried away."

"Damn it, Jessica, go—"

"I know. Go to sleep. I just want you to know that I think you're a very nice man. I'm glad to have you for a brother."

A brother, did she say? He'd almost made love to her and now she's paying him compliments? He almost asked her why, but maybe it was better that he didn't know.

Maybe she was thanking him for stopping when she asked. She didn't have to be so damned surprised. She must have had a really rotten idea of who he was if she had to compliment him for not taking advantage of their present situation.

Steve flopped over on his stomach and buried his head under the pillow.

Jessica lay awake for a long time that night reviewing all that had happened to her since she'd left New York. Who would have believed it? The idea of her going anywhere with Steve Donovan would have been laughed out of existence. To share his bed? To share a passionate kiss?

Never.

To have wanted to continue their lovemaking? What in the world was happening to her?

Was she brave enough, and honest enough, to find out? At this point, she wasn't at all sure.

Five

Jessica was brought out of a deep sleep the following morning by a firm swat on her derriere accompanied by a hearty voice announcing, "Rise and shine, princess. I was just informed that Johanson is having our breakfast delivered to our room. Considerate of him, I must say. He probably thinks we wore ourselves out last night and don't have the strength to manage the stairs."

A sudden dousing with a bucket of ice water could not have been more effective. Jessica rolled over and bolted out of bed. She stood beside her bed and faced the grinning man on the other side with a fury that had to be seen to be believed.

"What the hell do you think you're doing!"

Steve rested his hands on his hips and leisurely inspected the irate and rumpled woman before him. The same woman who had cost him several restless hours the night before. The same woman who had curled next to him in the early dawn coolness. The same woman that was causing him to feel all sorts of things that were definitely not what he needed to be feeling at the moment.

"Waking you up," he responded mildly, working to keep a sober demeanor. God, she looked like a Valkyrie warrior, magnificent in her rage. He could almost see the sparks flying from her hair. Steve had an almost uncontrollable urge to grab her and kiss her until her head spun.

Instead, he turned away and wandered over to the window. "I had no idea having to face breakfast first thing in the morning would upset you so." He glanced over his shoulder. "Shall I let them know that you would prefer to delay it for a while? How about if I just have them bring the coffee? Would that help? I should have guessed you were one of those people who doesn't feel human until after your first cup of coffee." He started toward the phone. "I should have thought about that. I'll just—"

"Don't touch that phone!"

"Despite what you may think, your highness, I'm not hard of hearing in the mornings. You can speak at a normal pitch and I'll be able to catch everything you say." He looked at her with his most innocent expression. "I don't know what you're so steamed up about. Would you have preferred that I kissed you awake?"

"Oooooh!" Jessica snatched up her robe, whirled and stalked into the bathroom, slamming the door.

Steve winced. Not the best beginning for the new day, he decided ruefully, even if he'd meant well. He heard the shower come on. Good idea. Maybe it would cool her down. He grinned, then started toward the door where he'd heard a soft tap.

Jessica stood under the hard driving water and ferociously washed her hair. Damn the man, anyway, looking so smug and attractive. What had he thought he was doing? Why couldn't he have called her name, or gently shook her, or— Slowly she began to calm down. She knew what was wrong even as she hated to admit it. He had disturbed her dreams all night with his flashing grin, his dancing eyes and the memory of his very seductive body pressed against hers. Every time she managed to rouse herself from one dream she would immediately fall back to sleep and dream of him again.

In her dream Steve had been holding her once more, murmuring soft words in her ear, his lips brushing against her skin causing shivers to run up and down her spine. Then to bring her rudely awake by popping her on her— She paused and rubbed the offended area.

By the time she stepped out of the shower Jessica had managed to calm down considerably. She was still drying off when Steve tapped on the bathroom door and asked, ''Would you like your coffee now, while you're dressing?''

She grabbed her robe and hastily tied it around her, then wrapped her hair in the towel. Cautiously she opened the door. He handed her a cup and saucer through the door, only his hand and forearm showing.

"Thank you," she muttered, striving for some graciousness but knowing that her tone needed a little more work.

"You're welcome."

She closed the door and took a sip of the coffee. Delicious. Absolutely delicious. She set the cup and saucer down and picked up the hair dryer that was lying on the counter. Obviously Mr. Johanson had thought of everything.

By the time she reentered her room she was in much better spirits. She actually smiled as she said, "Thanks again for the coffee."

"Do you want any breakfast? There's still plenty." Steve gestured at the table heavily laden with dishes and glassware.

"Whatever else he may be, I must say our host certainly knows how to treat his guests."

"Maybe he hopes that we'll forget we're here on an involuntary visit."

Jessica picked up a piece of bacon and took a bite. "Mmm. Maybe." She sat down at the table near the windows and reached for some fruit. Steve sat down once again. She tilted her head and looked at him. "Would you care to explain what that was all about this morning?"

"You slept through the phone ringing and my conversation with our host. So I figured that was the quickest way to get you awake." Steve grinned. "Besides, I figured since you consider me the nice, brotherly type I'd act accordingly."

"Did I say that? I must have been dreaming."

"No," he murmured, "that was later."

"What was later?" She looked at him suspiciously.

"When you were dreaming, running your hands across my chest and nibbling on my ear."

"I was not!"

He shrugged. "If you say so." He took another bite of food and picked up his glass of juice.

"I slept on my side of the bed the entire night."

"How do you know?"

"Because I was awake for most of it!"

"But not all."

"It's amazing how quickly I'm reminded of all the many reasons why I don't like you."

"Wow! If that's the way you kiss a man you don't like, I'd love to see your response to a man you care for. You probably create spontaneous combustion!"

Jessica found herself counting to ten, a habit that she'd resorted to with increasing frequency since Steve had come into her life.

"I think it most ungentlemanly of you to remind me of that kiss. I apologized for my behavior."

"So you did." Steve showed an inordinate amount of interest in his breakfast.

"It wasn't so surprising, really, that we should have responded so strongly to each other."

He glanced up. "Oh, really? And what is your theory about that? I'm sure you have one."

"We were both tired…and upset. All of this is really strange, you have to admit." Jessica waved her hand at the room.

"What's so strange about it?"

"You know what I mean. Here we are sharing a room, sleeping in the same bed."

"Speak for yourself," he muttered.

"What's that supposed to mean?"

"It means, your highness, that I didn't do much sleeping last night, either."

"Did I keep you awake?" She remembered trying to turn over as little as possible, hoping not to disturb him.

"You could say that" was his only response.

"Well, I'm sorry. I'm just not used to sleeping with someone."

"Do you think I am?"

Jessica stopped eating, her fork halfway to her mouth. With her thoughtful gaze on him, she pondered the question for a moment. "Yes," she finally said with a nod. "That's exactly what I think."

"Well, thanks a lot, princess."

She looked at him in surprise. "You're acting like I just insulted you."

"Give me a little credit for some discrimination, all right? And the fact that I stay relatively busy with my work. Or maybe you don't consider what I do work."

She grinned. "Mr. Johanson's comment about digging into other people's private lives hit home, didn't it?"

"When their so-called private lives jeopardize the lives of others, I consider it justified."

"But what you're doing could be dangerous, couldn't it?"

If she only knew the half of it! "Very rarely." Again, Steve spoke the truth. Much of what he did for both jobs was a tedious gathering of information. A comment here, a veiled remark there, taken alone oftentimes meant nothing, but when the information was compiled and assimilated with data gleaned from other agents, sometimes an amazingly accurate pattern became apparent.

Steve had been warned when he'd been recruited in school that the job was far from the glamorous picture painted in movies and novels, but what he was being asked to do could prove to be a valuable source of information for the government.

Because of his contacts he'd also been on top of breaking stories. He never released any information without prior approval from Max. He wouldn't jeopardize the security of the country in order to be first with a story.

Steve grinned at the thought. Max would string him up if he ever attempted to do so. There were several stories he'd investigated that hopefully would never reach the public.

"When are we going back to Sydney?"

"I understand Mr. Johanson has placed his car at our disposal."

"Well, I don't know about you, but I'm ready to get out of here."

"Oh, really? And here I thought you were secretly hoping that we'd have to share that bed for another night at the very least."

She smiled sweetly at him. "Dream on, big brother, dream on." She laughed when her comment made Steve frown.

By the time they were dropped off at her hotel later that afternoon, Jessica could find no fault with anything in her little world. Their guide was much more forthcoming with his comments on the return trip, patiently answering all of her questions about the countryside.

Steve spent the time reviewing what he had learned about Eric Johanson. He'd glossed over what had happened to them, but he was far from treating it lightly. As soon as he could get to a phone he considered safe, he was going to call Max and report what had happened. The first thing they needed to do was to run a check on Mr. Johanson and see what the international intelligence community could tell them about him.

Perhaps he was an eccentric millionaire who liked to keep tabs on the press that came in and out of the country. Then again, he might have some knowledge regarding the disappearance of Trevor Randall.

Obviously he hadn't been concerned over the possibility of receiving unkind press as a result of his actions. Perhaps he was used to the clout he could wield and assumed that Steve understood his power.

Steve certainly intended to find out a great deal more about Mr. Johanson and his peculiar way of greeting tourists.

Steve followed Jessica into the hotel. Luckily they were still holding her reservation.

"Are you still going to your hotel?" she asked, after she'd been given the key to her room.

"Yes. Why?"

She wasn't sure. She shrugged. "I just wondered."

"Are you afraid of staying here alone?"

"Of course not!"

"By the time you make contact with the people in the tourism business and get acquainted, you'll feel like a native."

"Of course."

They stood in front of the elevators looking at each other. Steve reached over and pushed the button and the elevator doors silently slid open.

"Your luggage has already gone to your room."

"Yes."

"So take care of yourself and have a good time."

"I will. You do the same."

"I will."

They continued to look at each other. The elevator doors slowly slid closed. Steve shook his head as though trying to clear it. "I, uh, if you want to, we might get together some night for dinner before you leave."

"I'd like that."

"All right. Then I'll give you a call in a day or two, just to see what your schedule is like. Maybe we'll set up something then."

She smiled. "I'll look forward to it."

He touched her cheek with his hand. "I'm glad to have had the chance to get to know you a little better, princess. I guess I have to agree with the twins—sissy can be a lot of fun to be around."

Jessica could feel her face flushing. "Except early in the morning when I'm awakened unexpectedly."

"Yeah, they forgot to warn me about that."

"Thanks for everything, Steve. Take care." She turned and pushed the button for the elevator again.

This time when the doors opened she stepped inside, gave a little wave, and pressed the button for her floor.

He watched until she disappeared from view, then turned and strode out to the street.

He had too much to do to be wasting time watching elevators. The first thing he had to do was to get in touch with Max and try to solve what was going on with Johanson before he mapped out his strategy to search for the missing Trevor Randall.

The place Steve found to stay was a small, out of the way apartment building, leasing fully furnished places on a weekly, as well as monthly basis. The austerity of the two rooms suited his needs as well as his mood.

A phone was provided but he chose a public one to make his initial contact. A scrambler device could be installed in his phone in the apartment if Max wanted him to continue with their original plan.

As he guessed Max did not accept Eric Johanson's sudden interest in Steve with mild good humor.

"I'll have him checked out right away," Max said, obviously taking notes from the questions he'd fired at Steve as soon as the name came into the conversation. "Next item. Who the hell is Jessica Sheldon and what are you doing traveling with her?"

"She's my stepsister. It was my bad luck to find out we were both going to be here at the same time. I got volunteered by the family to play escort."

"I've never known you to do anything you didn't want to do, Steve. You must be slipping."

Steve heard the hint of humor in Max's voice and decided he must be accepting the report without wanting heads to roll.

"Good point. I suppose I couldn't resist provoking the woman. She wasn't too enthused about my company, you see."

"So where is she now?"

"Tucked away in her hotel room, getting on with her plans for this trip."

"Have you met up with your contact yet?"

"Not yet. I wanted to talk with you to be sure everything is still set as planned."

"We'll check on Johanson. I'll give you a call as soon as we get some response."

"I'll be in touch," Steve responded, ending the call.

As soon as Steve returned to his apartment he decided to contact Jessica and give her his phone number. She might need him for something.

She answered on the first ring.

"H'lo?"

Her husky voice caught him off guard. He'd forgotten how seductive she sounded. His voice sounded more gruff than he intended when he responded. "This is Steve."

Her voice warmed. "Oh, hello. I'm so glad you called."

"You are? Why? What's wrong?"

She chuckled. "Nothing's wrong. I forgot to find out where you were staying, that's all."

He gave her the phone number. "Did you reset the appointments that you had to cancel?"

"Yes. For tomorrow."

"No plans for tonight?"

"No. An early meal and plans to go to bed shortly."

"I hope you sleep better. I'm sorry about last night."

There was a pause. "I'm not. I felt safe being there with you. Had I been alone I wouldn't have closed my eyes all night."

There was nothing that *he* felt safe in saying in response to that remark, so he said, "Guess I'll let you go, princess. Call me if you need me."

"I'll do that. Thanks for calling."

When Steve hung up he discovered that he was smiling. He and Jessica were actually getting along with each other. What a pleasant surprise. Unfortunately, he could not label his feelings as being brotherly, especially not after having spent the night with her.

The first thing he had to do was to stop thinking about her. He had a job to do and he'd better get his mind on it.

Steve called the number he'd been given while he was in London. When a voice answered he gave the message he was told to give. There was a pause, then he was given a series of numbers that he knew gave him the time and place of a meeting. He jotted them down and hung up.

After checking everything in his room to make sure there was nothing to show he was anything but a tourist on vacation, he left. Playtime was over.

Jessica went to bed early just as she planned. What she hadn't counted on was her inability to go to sleep.

Her thoughts kept turning to Steve and how different he seemed from the man she'd thought he was.

She had to admit to herself that she liked his sense of humor even when he was baiting her. His sharp intelligence intrigued her. She tried not to think about how his flashing smile and intense gaze affected her.

She forced herself to think about her plans for the next day. She had looked forward to doing the research necessary for her article. The time had come. She was frustrated to think that Steve had suddenly assumed more importance in her life at the moment, even though she knew it was only temporary. She'd probably only see him when he took her to dinner. After that their paths wouldn't cross again until the next family gathering.

Jessica forced her mind to quiet and eventually she drifted off to sleep.

When Steve returned to his room he was exhausted. He'd made connections with his contact who gave him some interesting leads. Trevor Randall had had several interesting hobbies that he could have chosen to pursue as a vocation in a new life. The question was how quickly could Steve find out if the man had in fact moved to Australia and if so, where he might have settled.

The thought of the tediousness of the investigation seemed overwhelming when he had gone without sleep for too long.

As soon as he reached his room Steve pulled out his key and started to insert it in the lock. Then he paused. Someone had been in the room since he had left. One of the reasons he preferred an apartment to a hotel was because no one was supposed to be in his room. He could monitor if anyone was interested in him.

Obviously someone was. He unlocked the door and opened it enough to flip on the light. Then he stepped inside. It didn't take long for him to discover that no one was there now. Whoever had been there was a professional. If Steve hadn't known what to look for there would have been no sign of entry.

Thoughtfully he prepared for bed. His room could have been checked for any number of reasons, none of which had anything to do with Trevor Randall. For all he knew Eric Johanson was having him followed.

Steve turned out the light and stretched out on the bed. What if it had something to do with Johanson? If so, he'd know that Steve wasn't spending his time with Jessica. Damn. He wished he'd thought of another story that had not involved her. Hopefully she'd be going home before long and he wouldn't have to worry about her involvement in this situation.

After a few hours' sleep he'd give Max a call and see what he'd turned up.

Steve sighed and rolled over onto his stomach. He was almost too tired to sleep. His mind kept flashing pictures. Instead of his job, he kept thinking about Jessica.

He groaned. He wished to hell he could get her out of his mind. Unfortunately that was not to be the case. His dreams were filled with her.

Six

Steve tried to block out the noise that kept disturbing his sleep but nothing worked. The pillow only muffled the insistent sound but could not stop it.

By the time he was awake enough to realize the phone beside the bed was ringing, he also discovered that his room was brightly lit with sunshine.

He fumbled for the receiver and dragged it to his ear. "Donovan."

"Oh, Steve. Hi. It's me, uh, Jessica. I was about to hang up."

Steve forced his eyes open and squinted at his watch. It was almost two o'clock. He hadn't gotten home until four in the morning and wasn't sure when he finally fell asleep. He hadn't meant to sleep the day away.

"I had a late night," he muttered. "Guess I over-slept." When she didn't say anything Steve said, "Jessica? You there?"

"I'm sorry if my calling you is inconvenient." Her regal tone was very much in evidence.

He grinned to himself. "I'll try to overlook it. So what's up?"

"I thought you would want to know that when I returned to the hotel just now, I found a message here. For you."

"For me? Who would call me there?"

"Mr. Johanson. He wants you to contact him."

Steve groaned. "What's with this character, any-way?"

"I have no idea."

"Hold on. I've got to find something to write with." Steve crawled out of bed and fumbled in his suitcase, found a pad and ballpoint pen and sat down by the phone. "Okay. What's his number?"

She gave it to him.

"How was your day?" he asked. "Meet any inter-esting people?"

"As a matter of fact, I did. Obviously you had no problems getting acquainted, either."

"What's that supposed to mean?"

"I was referring to your late night."

He chuckled at the icy tone. "I was working, prin-cess. How could I possibly look at another woman after all that we've shared together?"

"I am not amused."

He sighed. "I'm never my best when I'm suddenly awakened out of a sound sleep."

"I can certainly empathize. I seem to have the same problem."

"Mmm. But I don't think I would have minded if you were here to wake me up personally. Maybe we should conduct an experiment and see if I'd be in a better humor if I found you in bed with me."

There was a long silence that Steve interpreted to mean Jessica was considering hanging up on him. Not that he would blame her. He didn't know how she managed to bring out this side in him. He never talked to another woman the way he did her.

Since he hadn't heard a click, he decided to try to mend some fences. "Do you have any plans for this evening?"

"Yes." She gave him a prompt, crisp response.

"What kind of plans?"

"Gregory Phillips has kindly invited me to dinner and the theater. He said that everyone visiting Sydney must visit the Opera House while they're here. It's mandatory or something."

"Who's Gregory Phillips?"

"One of the people I met today. He has a travel bureau here."

"Oh."

"I've got to go, Steve."

"Sure. I'll talk to you later." He hung up the phone, frowning. He didn't like the sound of Jessica going out with someone she didn't know. Didn't she understand how vulnerable she was? Look how far from home she was. How did she know what kind of guy this Phillips was?

It would probably be a good idea if he showed up, just to let the man know she had somebody nearby that cared about her.

In the meantime, he needed to call Max and Johanson. He ran his hand through his hair. When had his life gotten so confusing? He'd never had so much trouble focusing on what needed to be done before. Jessica Sheldon was a distraction he didn't need at the moment, but he wasn't sure he could get her out of his mind.

As soon as Max answered Steve said, "Johanson wants me to call him. I don't know why. Do you?"

"Haven't a clue. So far everything we've uncovered on this guy is strictly legitimate. He earned his fortune through real estate. He's known as something of an eccentric."

"I'd certainly go along with that."

"Are you going to call him?"

"I doubt if I have any choice. Otherwise, he might take it into his head to offer us free but mandatory taxi service out to see him again."

Max snorted. "Find out anything at your end?"

"I showed the picture of Randall to my contact to verify. He says that he looks familiar to him, but he can't seem to place where he might have seen him."

"Then you really are on to something. I wasn't sure."

"Looks like it."

"Thought you'd sound happier."

"Guess I've got a lot of things on my mind at the moment. I'll get back to you."

Steve hung up and walked into the bathroom. He needed to shower and shave, get something to eat and try to decide what to do about Jessica.

Dinner was superb and the play was boisterously funny. Jessica thoroughly enjoyed both. However, she found to her disgust that her thoughts kept returning to Steve all evening, wondering what he was doing and with whom.

What frustrated her was that she cared. The man was not a part of her life. Why did she continue to think of him so often?

After the play, Gregory suggested they stop and have a drink somewhere. He was a charming companion and an absolute fountain of information for her article. Jessica found herself interviewing him, which he seemed to find amusing. He was more than willing to oblige.

After a drink he took her for a ride to enjoy the lights of Sydney. By the time they reached the hotel, Jessica was surprised to discover it was after one o'clock in the morning.

As they crossed the lobby she said, "Oh, Gregory, I'm so sorry. I didn't mean to keep you out so late."

"What nonsense. You don't owe me an apology. I have thoroughly enjoyed your company."

"I've enjoyed myself very much. The play was really funny. I can't remember when I've laughed so hard."

They stopped at the elevators. From the corner of her eye she saw someone approaching and glanced around.

"Steve! What are you doing here!"

Steve flashed his smile as he looked over the tall, blond man standing beside Jessica. "I had a message from the family, so I thought I'd drop by." Before she had a chance to respond he stuck out his hand. "You must be Phillips. Jessica mentioned she would be seeing you tonight."

Gregory looked at Jessica, then back to Steve. "I'm afraid you have the advantage, then. Jessica hasn't mentioned you."

"Oh, she's still a little miffed that our folks wanted me to keep an eye on her. She doesn't like the idea of big brother watching out for her."

"I see," Gregory said with a smile. "You're Jessica's brother."

"Steve," Jessica asked. "What sort of message do you have that couldn't have waited until morning?"

He dropped his arm around her shoulder. "Don't panic, now. Everything's all right." He glanced at Gregory. "You don't have to worry about seeing her to her room. I'll go on up with her."

Gregory nodded. "Whatever you say." He turned to Jessica. "I'll give you a call tomorrow, if that would be all right?"

The elevator doors opened and Steve nudged her into the elevator. Jessica barely had time to say, "I'd like that," before the doors closed between them. She jerked away from Steve. "What do you think you're doing?"

"Just looking after you, that's all."

"I am perfectly capable of looking after myself, you idiot. Gregory must think I'm a complete fool."

"Nonsense. He just knows that you have a big brother who cares about you."

The elevator stopped on their floor and they got out. When they got to her room he held out his hand for her key. She slapped it into his hand and he opened the door. She had left a small lamp on.

She marched past him. When she heard the door close she turned, her eyes flashing. "I wish you'd get off this big brother kick. I don't need you or anyone else looking after me. I'm doing just fine, thank you very much."

"All right. So I was wrong. Go ahead and hang me." He stood there, his back against the door, his hands on his hips.

Jessica spun away from him. "So what is this urgent message from home?"

"I just made that up. Actually, I wanted to tell you what Johanson wanted."

She sat down on the side of the bed and pulled off her shoes. Rubbing her toes she asked, "Why would you think I'd care?"

"Because it concerns you."

She glanced up. "Me?"

He grinned and wandered over to the window. "Yeah. Johanson was obviously impressed with you. I suppose he wants to help you out with your assignment."

She watched him warily. "How?"

"He's invited us to fly up to Queensland to visit one of his plantations in his private jet."

"You're kidding me."

"Nope. Thought it might help you with your article. I told him I'd check with you and get back to him tomorrow." He glanced at his watch. "Today."

"Did he say where?"

"His place is close enough to Port Douglas that we might have time to see the Barrier Reef. I told him you were on a very tight schedule and that we couldn't stay long. He seemed to accept that."

"I wonder what he's up to?" She got up and joined him at the window.

"Good question. He says he's promoting tourism, but I have a hunch he wants to keep his eye on me."

"Why?"

"I don't know, Jessica. Maybe to make sure I don't find the man I'm looking for. There's a lot going on right now that I don't understand." He turned to her. "For instance, I don't know why I was jealous of Gregory Phillips tonight."

Jessica heard what he said but couldn't believe that he'd said it. Steve jealous? Of her?

When she met his gaze she saw an expression she'd never seen before. His eyes had darkened and he looked almost grim.

"Steve?" she whispered.

He pulled her into his arms as though he could no longer fight the urge to hold her. "What the hell's happening to me?" he muttered. Then his lips found hers.

The kiss seemed to send a flaming jolt of electricity through her clear to her toes. Her knees quivered in reaction and Jessica felt as though her bones were starting to melt.

Still kissing her, Steve picked her up and carried her to the bed. It never occurred to Jessica to resist. Whatever caused the friction between them had managed to start a raging fire.

"I want you so much," Steve murmured when he finally drew back for air. "I feel like I was born with this ache inside of me, wanting you, needing you, waiting for you to appear in my life." His words were punctuated with soft kisses that he rained down upon her face. "You are driving me out of my mind."

Jessica felt dazed. How could he possibly believe she was intentionally doing anything? She could only hold him as his kisses seemed to break down the conditioning built up during her lifetime.

He unfastened her blouse, then reached for the front fastening of her lacy bra. As soon as he gently pushed aside that last covering he searched for and found the impudent tip of her breast. Eagerly his lips teased and tantalized her. Every new sensation created a response from deep within her.

His kisses seemed to rage out of control like a forest fire, starting new blazes wherever his lips touched until she felt as though she were a trembling mass of flames.

Jessica fumbled with the buttons on his shirt until she could place her hands on his bare chest. His response was all she could possibly hope for when she ran her fingers lightly across the muscled expanse.

When he raised his head to look at her, her eyes were closed, her lips curved into a smile.

Steve realized what he'd done; what he was in the process of doing. He was seducing Jessica . . . and she wasn't putting up any resistance.

He'd promised to look after her and protect her, but no one had thought about her need for protection from him.

With a groan that echoed around the room, he buried his head into the side of her neck, trying to gain some kind of control over himself.

Jessica slipped her hands around his body so that she was holding him tightly against her, his chest pressed against hers. She explored the muscles beneath her fingertips, loving the feel of him pressed against her.

He took several deep breaths, then slowly relaxed against her. She wasn't sure what had happened, but she knew that Steve had stopped making love to her. Instead, he now held her to him, possessively and firmly. She turned her head and kissed his ear. She felt him shudder.

"You okay?" she whispered.

He nodded but didn't speak.

They lay there in each other's arms for several long minutes before he finally said, "I need to go."

She nodded. "I suppose."

Slowly he came up on his elbows and looked down at her. "But I don't want to."

Jessica smiled at him. "I might as well be honest and admit that I don't want you to, either."

"I don't think it would be a very good idea for me to stay, do you?"

"No."

They looked at each other, then he slowly smiled. "It's hell being a responsible adult, isn't it?"

"Um-hmm."

He sat up and ran his hand through his hair. "So what should I tell Johanson?"

"Aren't you working on your assignment?"

"Yes, but I can't let you go to Queensland alone. It would give you additional information for your article, as he suggested, and I can manage a few days away."

"Then I'd like to go, if you think we'll be okay."

He cupped her chin in his hand. " I won't let anything happen to you, princess. Besides, I'd like to spend some more time with you, to continue to get to know you better."

She knew what he was saying. In the normal course of their lives they wouldn't see much of each other after this trip. Except for family gatherings, there would be no reason to keep in touch. She sighed.

"What's wrong?"

"We would never work out together."

He nodded. "I know."

"You're busy with your job. I'm busy with mine."

"I've already thought of that."

"It's not as though whatever's happening between us is a big romance, or anything. We've just got some sort of chemical reaction going on between us."

Steve buttoned his shirt. "We can deal with it."

She watched as he walked over to the door. "Yes."

"So I'll call Johanson and get back to you with the details."

Jessica propped herself on one elbow and smiled. "Fine."

He stood there for a few moments in silence, looking at her. Then he shook his head and muttered, "I've gotta get out of here." With a wave he turned and opened the door.

After Steve pulled the door closed behind him, Jessica slid off the bed and put on the night latch. She still felt bewildered by what had happened once again between them. She was even more bewildered by what had almost happened. Both of them knew that she had been willing, even eager, to continue their lovemaking.

She'd never felt so caught up in what she was feeling before in her life. She'd wanted him to make love to her. The revelation astounded her.

Would she ever forget the surge of pleasure that had run through her when he had admitted to being jealous? Had Steve recognized the same symptom in her that morning when she had called him and interpreted his late night to have meant that he had been with another woman?

Despite what Steve had said when Jessica had first arrived at the lake, there was a mutual admiration of sorts between them. Perhaps it had always been there and she had resisted accepting her reaction for what it was.

Jessica slowly undressed for bed and turned out the light. She walked over to the window and looked out at the lights that surrounded the Harbour. Here she was in Australia and all she could think about was Steve Donovan.

She ought to have her head examined.

Seven

The first thing Steve noted when he returned to his apartment was that no one had been there while he was out.

He went into the minuscule kitchen and made a pot of coffee. As soon as it was ready he poured a cup and sat down in the one comfortable chair to think.

He had come up with some surmises and now he needed to sort out the facts.

Fact No. 1: Eric Johanson. A man of wealth and obvious power if he had access to confidential visa information. A man afraid of something or he wouldn't feel threatened by a news reporter's visit to his country.

What was the man trying to hide? Why had he chosen to bring attention to himself by alerting Steve of his interest in Steve's visit? Had Steve managed to convince him that the visit was innocent? If he had not, would Johanson have been so willing to allow them to return to Sydney?

Why the offer to take them north? Public relations? Perhaps, but not likely.

Fact No. 2: Someone had thoroughly checked out Steve's room the night before. It was a professional job because nothing was disturbed. It didn't make sense that Johanson would have his things checked when he had ample opportunity of going through their belongings while they were guests in his home. Therefore, who else was interested in him and what were they looking for?

Fact No. 3: There was evidence to support the possibility that Trevor Randall had been seen in Australia recently, even though he was purported to have been killed five years ago.

His reasons for following the lead about Randall were simple. If he were alive, that was news and news was his business. In addition, if Randall were alive Max and the government agency Max represented wanted to know and would no doubt want to find out why his death had been faked.

Steve knew that his contact in Australia had been following leads for the last few weeks. Who had been alerted by the local agent's questions? Was Steve implicated by association with the local agent?

He got up and poured himself another cup of coffee. He had more questions than answers.

The decision he had to make at the moment was what to do about Johanson's invitation. On the surface, the offer seemed innocuous enough and it would be just what Jessica needed for her article.

Although he had played down his need to stay with his own investigation to Jessica, Steve felt that somehow, even though he couldn't find the connection as yet, Eric Johanson was tied to the reason Steve was there.

Did Johanson know Trevor Randall? Was he trying to provide a red herring to cover Randall's trail?

The questions kept floating around and around in Steve's mind.

He dropped his head against the back of the chair and sighed. Damn, he was tired. He'd lost track of the number of times he'd wished that Jessica wasn't involved in all of this, but nothing changed the fact that until she could get the information needed for her article she would be there.

There was no way he would allow her to go on Johanson's proposed excursion alone. He closed his eyes. There was nothing he could do at this point but go along and try to figure out Johanson's motives, look after Jessica and spend a large portion of his time taking cold showers.

He'd almost lost his control tonight and she hadn't helped much, melting against him as though she knew that they belonged together.

Kissing Jessica Sheldon could become addictive. Could be, hell; the woman was definitely a hazard to his peace of mind.

Steve pushed out of the chair and began to undress. He needed his rest. He couldn't let Johanson know that he was doing any more than enjoying a well-earned vacation.

He rubbed the back of his neck. Wait a minute. Maybe he could do a little more. If Johanson thought that Steve had an important meeting with members of the press, one at which Steve's absence would create all kinds of publicity, Johanson wouldn't try any funny stuff with them, and would make damn sure that Steve returned to Sydney on time. Johanson couldn't afford to take a chance, which would be added insurance for their safety.

After a quick shower that helped relax him somewhat, Steve turned out the lights. Immediately he thought of Jessica and how she had looked earlier in the evening. He could still smell the light floral fragrance she wore, feel her soft skin pressed against him, taste the sweet flavor of her breasts. He groaned and rolled over. How had she gotten to be an obsession with him in such a short time? He had to put her out of his mind. He had a job to do.

Even after he fell asleep, Steve's dreams were jumbled impressions of things he could do, had wanted to do, intended to do, with Jessica.

Jessica found Steve in the lobby when she came downstairs the next morning.

"Good morning," she said with a smile. "You look bright and cheerful this morning."

Steve knew exactly what he looked like and it was a far cry from bright or cheerful.

"Have you eaten?"

She nodded. "I had something sent up to the room. How about you?"

He shook his head.

Jessica checked her watch. "We're early. Mr. Johanson's car isn't due to arrive for another thirty minutes." She hooked her elbow through his and started toward the hotel restaurant. "Time enough to get some food in you."

The look he gave her would have intimidated a fainthearted person, but Jessica was made of stronger stuff, or so she tried to convince herself. At least he allowed her to lead him into the restaurant.

As soon as Steve had ordered, he looked at Jessica. "I can't recall ever having seen you in such a good mood. What gives?"

"Oh, no reason, really. It's a beautiful day, I'm going to have the privilege of being taken in a private jet to see part of the country I've always wanted to visit, and I'm getting paid at the same time." What she didn't want to admit was that she had awakened that morning with a sense of anticipation because she knew that she would be with Steve for the next few days.

At least she had been able to admit her feelings to herself. No one could take those feelings away from her. They were hers. Jessica knew that nothing could come of a relationship between the two of them, but for the next few days she could enjoy being with him, teasing him, learning more about him.

She smiled at him.

"Why don't I trust that smile?" Steve asked, an edge in his voice. He picked up his cup of coffee.

"I'm just being friendly."

IT'S FUN! IT'S FREE!
AND IT COULD MAKE YOU A
MILLIONAIRE

If you've ever played scratch-off lottery tickets, you should be familiar with how our games work. On each of the first four tickets (numbered 1 to 4 in the upper right)—there are PINK METALLIC STRIPS to scratch off.

Using a coin, do just that—carefully scratch the PINK STRIPS to reveal how much each ticket could be worth if it is a winning ticket. Tickets could be worth from $5.00 to $1,000,000.00 in lifetime money.

Note, also, that each of your 4 tickets has a unique sweepstakes Lucky Number...and that's 4 chances for a **BIG WIN!**

FREE BOOKS!

At the same time you play your tickets for big cash prizes, you are invited to play ticket #5 for the chance to get one or more free book(s) from Silhouette. We give away free book(s) to introduce readers to the benefits of the *Silhouette Reader Service*™.

Accepting the free book(s) places you under no obligation to buy anything! You may keep your free book(s) and return the accompanying statement marked "cancel." But if we don't hear from you, then every month we'll deliver 6 of the newest Silhouette Desire® novels right to your door. You'll pay the low members-only price of just $2.24* each—a savings of 26¢ apiece off the cover price—plus 69¢ for shipping and handling!

Of course, you may play "THE BIG WIN" without requesting any free book(s) by scratching tickets #1 through #4 only. But remember, the first shipment of one or more book(s) is FREE!

PLUS A FREE GIFT!

One more thing, when you accept the free book(s) on ticket #5 you are also entitled to play ticket #6 which is GOOD FOR A VALUABLE GIFT! Like the book(s) this gift is totally free and yours to keep as thanks for giving our Reader Service a try!

So scratch off the PINK STRIPS on all your BIG WIN tickets and send for everything today! You've got nothing to lose and everything to gain!

Here are your BIG WIN Game Tickets, worth from $5.00 to $1,000,000.00 each. Scratch off the PINK METALLIC STRIP on each of your sweepstakes tickets to see what you could win and mail your entry right away. (See official rules in back of book for details!)

This could be your lucky day - GOOD LUCK!

THE BIG WIN

TICKET 1
Scratch PINK METALLIC STRIP to reveal potential value of this ticket if it is a winning ticket. Return all game tickets intact.

LUCKY NUMBER

1I 857561

THE BIG WIN

TICKET 2
Scratch PINK METALLIC STRIP to reveal potential value of this ticket if it is a winning ticket. Return all game tickets intact.

LUCKY NUMBER

3Q 859203

THE BIG WIN

TICKET 3
Scratch PINK METALLIC STRIP to reveal potential value of this ticket if it is a winning ticket. Return all game tickets intact.

LUCKY NUMBER

5N 857326

THE BIG WIN

TICKET 4
Scratch PINK METALLIC STRIP to reveal potential value of this ticket if it is a winning ticket. Return all game tickets intact.

LUCKY NUMBER

9T 856709

FREE BOOKS

TICKET 5
We're giving away brand new books to selected individuals. Scratch PINK METALLIC STRIP for number of free books you will receive.

AUTHORIZATION CODE

130107-742

FREE GIFT

TICKET 6
We have an outstanding added gift for you if you are accepting our free books. Scratch PINK METALLIC STRIP to reveal gift.

AUTHORIZATION CODE

130107-742

YES! Enter my Lucky Numbers in THE BIG WIN Sweepstakes and tell me if I've won any cash prize. If PINK METALLIC STRIP is scratched off on ticket #5, I will also receive one or more FREE Silhouette Desire® novels along with the FREE GIFT on ticket #6, as explained on the opposite page.

(C-SIL-D 07/90) 326 CIS 816V

NAME _____

ADDRESS _____ APT. _____

CITY _____ PROVINCE _____ POSTAL CODE _____

Offer limited to one per household and not valid to current Silhouette Desire® subscribers.
©1990 HARLEQUIN ENTERPRISES LIMITED

PRINTED IN U.S.A.

Carefully detach card along dotted lines and mail today!

Play *all* your BIG WIN tickets and get everything you're entitled to— including FREE BOOKS and a FREE GIFT!

Canada Post
Postes Canada
125

"So I see. Somehow I find that totally out of character for you, at least as far as I'm concerned."

"I suppose I have been a little rough on you, haven't I?"

"Not if your intention was to keep me avoiding you."

"Ah, but you haven't avoided me. Instead, you saw my behavior as a challenge. If I'd known how you deal with challenges, I would have chosen another way to behave towards you."

Steve studied her in the morning light. Her fair skin glowed with a translucent sheen that no makeup could duplicate. Her eyes sparkled as though she was delighted with the world and all God's creatures. She looked beautiful and very desirable.

He frowned. He didn't need to be reminded of just how desirable he found her.

Steve felt relieved when his breakfast was set before him and he made short work of it. Jessica seemed content to sit there with him and watch the people who came in and out of the restaurant.

He felt a little more mellow after he'd eaten. He'd skipped his evening meal the night before. It was amazing how eating could change a person's attitude.

"There's Frick and Frack," Jessica said in a low voice.

"Who?" Steve stared at her in surprise before looking toward the door.

"Mr. Johanson's messengers."

He grinned at the names, then rose and walked around to help her from her chair.

"My, my. A real gentleman. I feel so cherished."

"I think I liked you better when you were determined not to ever talk to me."

"Oh. Well, if I were trying to gain your admiration, I suppose I'd take heed of that statement."

He shook his head but couldn't withhold the smile. "Has anyone ever told you that you have a smart mouth?"

"On occasion, but I usually considered the source and decided they were too sensitive."

He began to laugh. They arrived at the spot where the two men stood waiting.

"Good morning," Jessica said sunnily. "Are you supposed to take us to the airport?"

"Yes."

The four of them walked through the lobby and out to the limousine waiting for them. Steve gave a brief prayer of thanksgiving that Jessica decided not to spread her good cheer to the other two. He wasn't at all sure they would be able to handle her peculiar form of humor. He wasn't sure he could, for that matter. And he had a better understanding of the woman—he hoped.

For the next few days they were going to have to pretend to be lovers enjoying themselves in the Land of Oz. He'd had worse assignments, but none that would put quite the same strain on him as being Jessica's lover in public and a brother in private. Perhaps it would have helped him relate if he'd had a sister his own age. The twins could have been his children so he couldn't relate to them other than as an adult to a child.

A thought suddenly occurred to him. The twins could be his and Jessica's children. David and Diane looked enough like them they could pass as their own offspring. The thought of having children with Jessica sent a bolt of shock coursing through him.

"Didn't you get any sleep last night?"

Steve had placed sunshades over his eyes as soon as they had walked into the sunlight. He turned and looked at Jessica from behind darkened lenses. "Why do you ask?"

She looked at him as though she couldn't believe he needed to ask. "Well, it could be because your eyes looked bloodshot and the lines in your face could have been caused by a convoy of trucks. Or the fact that you appear to have fallen asleep sitting up. Or—"

"All right. I get the message. I just had trouble sleeping."

"Want to talk about it?" Jessica asked in a low voice. The two men in the front seat had the window closed between them and were obviously unable to hear their conversation.

"I don't need an analyst, thanks all the same."

"Are you sorry you decided to go on this jaunt?"

"I'm sorry for a lot of things. This trip is only a small part of it."

"Are you sorry you have to be with me?"

When Steve didn't answer Jessica bit her lower lip and looked away. Finally, in a suspiciously husky voice, she said, "I thought we were getting along much better."

"That's the problem," he muttered to himself.

"What?"

"I said—" he paused and cleared his throat "—that I've been forced to put some work on hold and I'm concerned."

"Then why didn't you tell Johanson no?"

"Because I want to know what's behind his invitation."

"Maybe he's just being nice to a couple of tourists."

He looked at her for a moment before he replied. "Do you still write Santa every year and leave carrots for the reindeer on Christmas Eve?"

Jessica couldn't remember ever having known a more exasperating man. "All right, then. Why did he go to all the trouble to plan this trip for us?"

"Perhaps so he would know where we are."

"Why would he care?"

"Now that is a question worthy of contemplation. Why don't we spend the remainder of our time to the airport considering that question?" She started to say something and he held up his hand. "In silence. We can always compare notes later."

That certainly did the trick, Steve decided after a few minutes of glacial-like quiet. Maybe his salvation on the trip would be to keep her so angry at him that she wouldn't allow him within ten feet of her.

In the meantime, he would do just as he suggested. Try to figure out why Johanson wanted to keep an eye on them.

The road they were on as they drew near to the airport took them to another section of the airstrip. They continued on the concrete and stopped near a small, sleek-looking plane. Jessica knew nothing about jets or other aircraft, but she was impressed with the looks of this one.

As soon as the car stopped the door opened and Jessica climbed out. She ignored Steve as much as possible, which was difficult because he had immediately wrapped his arm around her waist and pulled her against his side as he started toward the plane.

"Is Mr. Johanson here?" he asked one of the men.

"No. He had some business to attend to in Queensland and needed to be there earlier this morning. He sent the jet back to pick you up."

"Thoughtful of him," Steve said with a smile.

There was no answering smile.

The interior of the plane looked like someone's idea of a flying carpet, filled with cushioned splendor. Steve and Jessica sat down and strapped themselves in. There was a quiet conference between one of the men who had picked them up and the pilot. Then he stepped off the plane and the pilot made sure the door was securely fastened.

He gave Steve and Jessica a pleasant smile, mentioned how long they would be in the air and disappeared up front.

Jessica made a point of picking up a magazine and flipping through it rather than try to establish any conversation. Steve had certainly made himself quite clear about her attempts to build an open, friendly relationship.

She wished she had the courage to confront him about his behavior last night. He certainly hadn't seemed to mind communicating with her then! The communication had been mostly nonverbal, but he had still managed to make himself understood quite clearly.

A responsible adult, was he? Is that the way he viewed his actions? All she saw were the double messages he kept sending her! *Stay away from me while I hold and kiss you like a person intent on devouring you.*

The problem was that she now had a taste of what it would be like to have Steve Donovan make love to her. Her imagination hadn't been able to come up with anything to compare with the actual event.

Obviously what they had shared had not been anything special to Steve, for if it had, he wouldn't be behaving in such a distant manner toward her today. Jessica leaned back and closed her eyes, feeling the surge of power that would soon lift them into the air.

"Nervous?" Steve asked, touching her hand that was clenched around the armrest.

She wondered what had been his first clue: the fact that all of her blood had rushed to her feet, probably leaving her face white, or the fact that her nails were imbedded in the arms of the chair.

"A little," she admitted, refusing to look at him.

He took her hand between both of his and rubbed it gently.

Why did he have to be so contrary? Just as she had managed to convince herself that she truly hated Steve Donovan and wanted nothing further to do with him, he had the audacity, the absolute gall, to be loving and gentle with her.

The sudden rush of blood caused by her rising temper felt wonderfully renewing. She was not going to faint after all. She'd have a stroke maybe, but not faint.

Since Steve had arranged for Jessica to sit by the window, he continued to lean close to her to see where they were.

"Would you like to change seats?" she finally asked, after the whiff of his after-shave drifted past her for the third time.

"Aren't you enjoying the view?"

"Well, yes, I am. I just thought you'd be able to see better."

"I can see fine," he drawled, his gaze wandering over her face as though memorizing each feature.

"Would you stop that!"

"Stop what?"

"Looking at me like that!"

"Like what?"

"Like I was your favorite flavor of ice cream and you were trying to decide where to start!"

Steve threw back his head and laughed.

His laugh was infectious and Jessica could no longer hide her enjoyment of watching and listening to him. Damn the man, anyway. He was managing to wrap her around his little finger and she didn't like it—not one bit. She found it hard to resist him when he was in this mood.

When the plane started its descent they both glanced out. Rolling green hills lay below.

"It's really beautiful, isn't it?" Jessica murmured.

"Yes."

By the time they landed at the private airfield and stepped from the plane, Jessica felt that she had been whisked to a truly magical land. Giant fern palm and banyan trees skirted the open area. Vines with crimson and orange blooms hung from the towering trees and bushes.

Mr. Johanson waited for them in a utility truck.

"Welcome to Queensland," he remarked while Steve and Jessica climbed into the back.

"It is truly beautiful," Jessica said, looking around her.

Eric smiled. "I'm glad you can appreciate why I come up here whenever I get the chance."

"I've never seen such a varied collection of flowers blooming in the wild."

"Wait until you see my formal gardens. Why, they rival the botanical gardens of any of the large cities."

Steve studied the older man, noticing his relaxed and genial air. For the first time he wondered if paranoia had taken over his thinking. Although he didn't care for Johanson's strong-arm tactics when they had first arrived, he couldn't fault him for lack of courtesy and consideration since that time.

Max had said Johanson was known as an eccentric. Perhaps that was all that had set Steve off. He was used to dealing with conniving people. Perhaps he looked for intrigue where there was none.

He could only bide his time and wait to see what happened next.

Eight

The road they followed from the landing strip continued to climb into the surrounding hillside. When at long last they broke from the trees, Jessica gasped. They were on a ridge overlooking a fertile, green valley surrounded by mountain peaks. Nestled in the valley was a colonial-style home set in the midst of a profusion of color. A wide veranda encircled the house.

They pulled up in front of the gate in a white picket fence that bordered the property. Jessica couldn't believe the place was real. The house looked as though it had appeared like magic on a dimensional plane that might cause it to disappear back into its own time at any moment.

A large, wide hallway ran from the front of the house to the back, with rooms on both sides. A stairway led up to the second floor with a similar floor plan. Her excitement at being able to see such a beautifully well-preserved piece of history came to a sudden halt when their luggage was taken into one of the front upstairs bedrooms. Why hadn't she thought about the fact that Johanson would expect her to share a room with Steve? She looked at Steve for guidance but he was politely listening to their host's description of the area and how the house came to be built.

As soon as Johanson left them Jessica turned to Steve. "I don't think this is a very good idea."

He'd walked over to the window and was looking outside when she spoke. He glanced around. "What are you talking about?"

"Our sharing a room."

"Isn't it a little late to be thinking about that now?"

"Couldn't we tell him that we need separate rooms?"

"I could, but I'm not going to."

"Why not?"

"Because I don't know what he's up to and I don't trust him. I'll feel much better keeping you as close to me as possible."

She glanced at the bed in question. It was much smaller than the one they had shared in the Blue Mountains.

"Oh, I'll be close, all right."

What a little wretch, Steve thought. "I'll admit that it's more difficult to sleep with you next to me, my love, but I am more than willing to forgo my rest in favor of other pastimes."

Steve had the satisfaction of watching Jessica's face flame with rosy color.

By the time they had finished with their evening meal, their host had shown them around the house and garden and answered their questions about its history. Jessica seemed delighted and took copious notes and made rough sketches. No doubt she would return to the States with enough information for a book, Steve thought with concealed annoyance.

He stood on the steps and looked out over the garden. Johanson had told them that he had several men who worked full-time to keep the grounds looking so well. One of them was just now putting away his tools into a shed near the back fence. The wide hat he wore no doubt protected him from the tropical sun.

Steve turned away. He felt restless and edgy. Jessica seemed to have forgotten Johanson's earlier treatment of them and was chatting away with him as though they were old friends.

It suddenly struck Steve that he was as jealous of Eric Johanson's attention toward Jessica as he had been of her travel bureau friend. No doubt about it. He was losing his mind.

Long after Jessica went upstairs to bed, Steve stayed downstairs. For a while he talked with Eric. He noticed that the older man was excellent at parrying Steve's questions, as well as casually phrasing pertinent questions of his own. Steve concluded Eric was a formidable opponent and one that he would prefer to leave alone.

He hoped he would have that choice.

It was after midnight before he finally left his seat on the veranda and went upstairs. After Eric had finally given up with his subtle interrogation and gone to bed, Steve had wandered outside and watched as a storm gathered on the horizon and moved toward them. Strong wind carrying heavy rain drove him inside.

When he reached the top of the stairs he heard a rhythmic banging coming from the room assigned to him and Jessica. He quietly opened the door and went inside. The flapping of a loose window shade beat a tattoo against the window ledge. Glancing over toward the bed, he wasn't surprised to find Jessica sound asleep.

Steve grinned to himself and quietly walked over to the window where the rain was beating in. He closed it and adjusted the shade. He walked over to the bed and looked at Jessica.

She lay on her side, her hair fanned out on the pillow, her hand tucked under her chin. Not for the first time he noticed the resemblance between Jessica and Diane. Jessica didn't look much older than her baby sister at the moment. A flood of tenderness swept over him as he stood there, watching her sleep. How could he possibly deny his feelings for this beautiful, irritating, fascinating, provoking woman?

Steve finally had to admit to himself what he'd been denying for some time. He loved her. He'd loved her for a long time, rationalizing his feelings by attributing his confusion to the warmth he felt for her mother and the tenderness and love he had for the twins.

What he felt for Jessica was different. In addition to feeling a combination of warmth, tenderness and love, Steve also experienced a sense of understanding, need and strong desire.

He was unsure of what to do about it. For the moment, he would do nothing. There was too much going on. He would have to put his feelings for Jessica out of his mind and heart until after their present excursion.

Reluctantly he undressed and crawled into bed beside her. She turned toward him and he slipped his arm beneath her head, pillowing her against his shoulder.

She sighed and relaxed against him. Steve lay awake for a long time, listening to the storm, ever aware of the woman he held in his arms.

Later the next day, Steve reminded himself of his resolve of the night before. The problem was that once he had acknowledged to himself how he felt about her, he found it more difficult to control his reactions around her.

After their noon meal, he and Jessica decided to go for a walk. Eric cautioned them not to wander far, explaining that the bush was quite easy to become lost in. Jessica dug out a pair of well-worn jeans that fit her more snugly than Steve found particularly comfortable, especially as he was forced to follow behind her on the narrow trails.

He'd carefully done nothing to mar her good spirits today. He just wanted to enjoy her; he wanted to watch her enjoyment of everything around her. Today he wanted to forget who he was, who she was and just allow them to spend a few hours in each other's company.

By the time they stopped at the little stream that crossed the barely discernible path they followed, they were both a little winded.

"I can't believe this place," Jessica said, splashing the water over her wrists and cheeks. "It's like a fairy wonderland." She pointed high above them. "Can you see the rainbow that's formed in the waterfall?"

She was right. They could be hundreds of miles from any sign of civilization. The place looked as untouched as the day it had been created.

Jessica sank down on a fallen log and looked around. "I hope you've been keeping track of where we are and how to get back."

"I thought you had."

She stopped digging in her knapsack for a can of juice. "You're kidding, right?"

Steve grinned. "A little, maybe. But I'm not at all sure I could find the same paths we followed. I do know the general direction we came from."

"Thank God. One of us needs to recall our scouting skills and I always flunked mine."

"You were a Girl Scout?"

"Don't look so disbelieving. Of course I was. Not that I managed to earn many badges, but I certainly worked at it." She looked at him. "How about you?"

"Oh, for a couple of years. We did the usual—backpacking, hiking and camping."

"Did you enjoy it?"

"Not particularly. How about you?"

She laughed. "Same here."

He looked around the small clearing. "So what are we doing here, *Kimo sabe*?"

She grinned at him and warbled, "Say, Mr. Custer, I don't want to go." They both laughed. "You have to admit that scouting was never done in surroundings like these." She waved her arms wide.

Steve sat there looking at Jessica for several moments in silence. "I've enjoyed being with you today."

She smiled. "I'm glad. I never know what kind of mood you're going to be in. I suppose it depends on what side of the bed you get up on."

He shook his head. "No. I've discovered the only bed I ever want to get out of is yours. Once I finally admitted that to myself last night, I quit fighting the overwhelming feelings I have for you."

Jessica stared at him in shocked surprise. She wanted to pinch herself to make sure she wasn't dreaming. Or maybe her hearing was going. Steve couldn't have said what she just thought she heard.

"Steve—"

Her sudden move toward him saved her life. Bark flew from the tree just behind her, right where her head had been a couple of seconds before. The crack of a rifle echoed immediately afterward, by which time Steve had tackled Jessica and rolled with her into the deep underbrush.

Another crack sounded and the foliage all around them seemed to fall like snowflakes. "Let's get out of here," he demanded, grabbing her arm and pulling her deeper into the dense growth.

Another fallen log lay on its side and he pulled her behind it, making sure that she was fully hidden.

Jessica's head was whirling. What had happened? What was going on? Was someone actually shooting at *them*? She felt disoriented as though she'd been popped into a nightmare of some sort without warning.

She glanced around for Steve and received her second shock. He was crouched beside her, watching the path they'd recently left, a pistol in his hand.

She must be dreaming. That was the only explanation her rational mind could come up with on such short notice. Where would Steve have gotten a gun? If he'd had it in his luggage they would have arrested him. Besides, what reason would he have for carrying one?

She could only crouch there behind the giant log and stare at him in bewilderment. Without looking at her, he said, "We've got to get away from here before whoever he is comes looking for us."

"Who is it?"

Steve slowly came to his feet, still bent over, and urged her into the deeper brush. "I'm not in the mood to stay around and find out, princess. Let's go."

Jessica lost all sense of time and direction. All she knew was that for what seemed like hours Steve dragged her into the deepest thickets and over the least likely looking paths. By the time he found the narrow dry gully between towering cliffs, Jessica was too exhausted to do more than stumble along behind him.

He had never let go of his hold on her wrist and she knew she would have bruises where his fingers had dug into her skin. But so what? She had so many scratches and bruises on other parts of her anatomy, a bracelet of blue-green flesh would successfully coordinate the various colors of her skin.

Jessica realized she must be losing control of her sanity if she was picturing herself in a fashion parade.

Steve came to a sudden stop, causing Jessica to plow into his back. He was staring up the face of the cliff. "If we could get up there, we'd be safe. I could watch for whoever came along looking for us."

She stared at the wall, then at him. "Are you out of your mind?"

"No. Look." He pointed out the roughness of the rock. "There are plenty of hand and toeholds. About twelve feet up, there looks to be a cave of some sort."

"What if it's already occupied?"

"We'll have to take that chance."

"Fine. You take your chance in the cave. I'll take my chance down here."

Steve turned around and looked at Jessica for the first time since they'd started their trek. She looked as though she'd been dragged through the bush. Come to think of it, that's exactly what had happened to her. But it was a hell of a lot better than being a target for some idiot.

Whoever had shot at them had been a skilled marksman. Only Jessica's sudden move and his quick reflexes had saved them for now.

"Come on. You only need to take a few steps and you can pull yourself the rest of the way."

"That's all right. You can go first."

"Damn it, Jessica. I want you up there first, so I'll know you're safe." She just looked at him. "Oh, hell. All right. We'll go up together. But if you slip, I won't be able to catch you."

"Then I'll make sure that I don't slip. How's that?"

Steve shook his head, then led her over to the cliff face. After pointing out handholds, he moved over a couple of feet and began to climb. He glanced back to find her still looking at him. "Hurry up."

Another two feet up and he could see in the cave. It was shallow. More important, it was empty. He glanced around. "All right, Madam Explorer, your fears are for naught. The cave's empty." He found another handhold and pulled himself onto the ledge in front of the cave. He looked at Jessica. She hadn't moved.

"Jessica, if I have to come back down there and carry you up here, I will, but believe me, you won't like me very much if I do."

"Whatever gave you the idea I liked you at all, Steve Donovan. This is not my idea of a fun vacation."

"Yeah, well, being shot at isn't one of my favorite sports, either, your highness. Now, get up here!"

He glared at her. She glared back. Then she thought she heard a rustling in the direction from which they had just come. She scaled the wall like a professional mountain climber working against the clock. "Did you hear something?" she gasped, throwing herself onto the ledge beside him.

He looked at her, not bothering to hide his grin. "My, my, princess. You have definitely been hiding some of your major talents. You're going to have to show me how you managed to do that so quickly.''

Jessica glanced down at the steep cliff she'd just scaled and swallowed. ''It's amazing what fear will do, isn't it?'' she finally managed to say despite the lump in her throat.

He turned away and crawled into the cave. It went back farther than it had first appeared, at least giving them enough room to stretch out full-length, even though they could not stand upright in it.

Steve leaned back against the side of the cave and fought the adrenaline that still coursed through him. Damn, but that had been close. He'd been forced to hide in various parts of the world in the most primitive of surroundings, from jungles to high mountain peaks, but he couldn't say that it was truly his favorite pastime.

Thank God they each carried a knapsack with food. Not much, but enough to get them by if they had to be out overnight. He leaned out and looked up, trying to see the sky. They had been moving in deepening shadow for some time but he hadn't taken the time to think about it. Here in the shadows of the cave where they hid, it was almost dark. And it would have to stay that way. They couldn't afford a light.

Jessica crawled in beside him. ''What are we going to do?''

''Eat something, get some rest and wait.''

''What are we waiting for?''

''To see what happens next.''

''What if nothing happens?''

"I'll be very surprised."

She sighed. What a pain he was. Which reminded her of something else. "Where did you get that gun?"

"Pistol."

"Whatever."

"A friend loaned it to me."

"What friend?"

"A true, loyal and obviously knowledgeable one. He said I might need it. He could be right."

"Where did you meet him?"

"In Sydney."

"You mean, you just met some guy who offered you a gun—all right, a pistol—and you took it, just like that?"

"I offered to pay for it, but he told me I could return it later."

"Steve, that's not what I mean and you know it. What kind of a guy would offer to loan you a lethal weapon?"

"One who was afraid I might need some protection."

"From Mr. Johanson?" she asked, disbelievingly.

"From whomever. We don't know who's practicing their marksmanship skills."

"I feel like I just walked into the middle of some ridiculous intrigue-adventure movie without a clue as to what's happening."

"Honey, in a movie you don't have to worry about becoming part of the action."

"I know that." Jessica stared at Steve sitting there against the wall, his knees bent, his arms crossed over his knees, looking as though he was resting up from an afternoon neighborhood scrimmage. "Steve?"

"Hmm." He'd leaned his head against the wall with his eyes closed.

"I'm scared."

"I know."

"But you aren't."

He opened his eyes, but he didn't say anything.

"You're acting as if this was all a routine exercise for you."

He still didn't say anything.

"You weren't even particularly surprised that someone shot at us."

"I wouldn't say that."

"Well, you certainly knew what to do to get us out of danger."

He watched her warily. "My scout training coming back to me, maybe?" he suggested.

"Wrong."

"So what do you think it is?"

"You've had some experience at keeping yourself alive."

"True."

"So what is it, Steve? Are you a drug smuggler? Arms? Mercenary for hire? What do you *really* do for a living?"

She'd run through the list as though she was used to associating with people in those fields on a regular basis, as though their conversation was taking place at a cocktail party or a trendy Manhattan night spot.

"Good God, Jessica. Give me a little more credit than that, all right? What do you know about drug and arms smuggling, anyway?"

She shrugged. "It's in every newspaper and magazine on the stands these days. Drugs and the money they generate seem to dominate the news."

"That doesn't mean that I'm involved with them, or anything else illegal, for that matter. I can't believe you'd accuse me of something like that." He sighed and shook his head. "Why should I be surprised? I should be used to you by now."

"What do you mean by that remark?"

"Nothing. It's just that you've got to have one of the most quirky minds of anyone I've ever known."

"Quirky?"

"Quirky."

"As in peculiar?"

"As in eccentric."

"Oh."

Silence held forth as the light gradually faded until they could no longer see each other.

"Steve?"

"Hmm?"

"I'm hungry."

"So eat."

"I lost my knapsack while you were dragging me through the forest earlier."

"Bush."

"What?"

"The Australians call this the bush, not forest."

"Do you want me to go look for my knapsack?"

"Great idea. Or better yet, why don't you ask whoever's tailing us to bring it along with him?"

"How do you know anyone's following us?"

"I know."

"How would he know where we went?"

"We left a trail as clear as one made by a Mack truck."

"So what do we do now?"

She heard him move but she couldn't see him. His hand touched her foot, then felt along her leg until it reached her knee.

"I would love to know what the hell you think you're doing now, studying anatomy by the Braille system?"

"You don't sound very scared to me." He found her hand that was resting on her knee and put a sandwich in it.

"I always sound mad when I'm scared." She unwrapped the sandwich and took a bite. It was heavenly.

"You must go through life being scared most of the time, then."

Oh, how she would love to see his face after having the nerve to be so insulting. "Actually, I only act this way around you."

"You're scared of me?" he asked, his surprise evident.

She took two more bites, chewed them very carefully before swallowing, then responded, "No more than you're scared of me."

"I'm terrified of you," he replied promptly.

She began to choke. He slid his arm around her shoulder and began to pound on her back until she shoved him away. He fumbled in his knapsack and found a can of juice. He pulled the tab off and placed it in her hand. She took several long swallows.

"Would you like to explain your last remark?" she finally managed to say hoarsely.

"No, I don't think so. At least not right now." After a beat of time, he added. "Maybe later."

She heard him moving around. "What are you doing?"

"Taking off my jacket. We might as well get as comfortable as possible. We'll have to wait for light before we try to get out of here."

"Do you really expect me to sleep here in a cave with someone hunting us down to try to kill us?"

"Suit yourself. I doubt that he's looking now that it's dark."

"I don't believe this," she muttered.

After what seemed to Jessica to be at least an hour of silence she finally spoke.

"Steve?"

"Hmm."

"Are you asleep?"

"Yes."

"How can you sleep?"

"Easy."

"I'm really frightened. What are we going to do?"

"Why don't you lie down here beside me? I'll hold you close and make you feel safe. That's the least that a possible drug/arms smuggling mercenary could do for you."

The idea didn't sound half bad to her. There were night noises outside like she'd never heard before. Strange sounds made by animals she knew she'd never seen before. They were in a foreign country, no matter how friendly and open the people were. Anything could be out there. For that matter, they might be occupying something's bed. What if it showed up expecting to find its home empty and they were there?

She made a dive toward the sound of Steve's voice and managed to land on top of him. She wrapped her arms around his neck and buried her head in his chest. There was no way she could hide her trembling.

"You're okay, princess. I promise I won't let anything get you, man or beast."

She hugged him tighter.

His arms came around her slowly, as though he was reluctant to touch her.

"I just don't know who's going to protect you from me," he finally said, lifting her chin and finding her quivering mouth with his.

Nine

Jessica could feel the heavy thudding beat of Steve's heart. She could feel the warmth of his large, strong body pressed against her. She couldn't get close enough to the warmth and the safety that he represented.

She returned his kiss with passion intensified by fear. As she clung to him, his gentle kiss soothed and steadied her.

"You're going to be fine, princess. Just fine. Try to relax now." His low, soothing words reached that part of her that had panicked from all that she'd experienced in the past few hours.

With a shuddering sigh, she loosened the tight grip she had around his neck. He turned slightly so that her body slid to the hard surface of the cave. But he did not let go of her. He ran his hands over her in long, comforting strokes.

Jessica found herself placing small, light kisses along his cheek and jaw and the corner of his mouth, while she imitated his touches. He felt so good to her, safe and secure. She slid her hand down his chest, glorying in the strength there. His shirt was in her way and she worked the buttons loose, pulling the shirt out of his pants.

When it fell open she sighed with pleasure, touching him lightly, smoothing the dark hair that matted his chest. With the tip of her tongue she lightly touched one of his nipples. His body jerked as though he'd just been electrocuted.

"Jessica!"

"Hmmmm." She kissed the nipple she had just touched, then delicately licked it.

"Do you have any idea what you're doing?" His voice sounded strangled.

"Umm-hmm." She began a trail of kisses downward, pausing at his navel to explore.

Steve leaned back from her, but could see nothing in the blackness. He felt as though his body had just been torched. He burned, the heat radiating from him so that he wondered how she could continue to touch him without being singed.

"You're driving me insane," he finally managed to say in a hoarse voice.

"Good," was her only reply.

Jessica continued her explorations. Steve fumbled in an attempt to push her away. His hand touched her breast and he froze. With an unsureness that he had never felt before, he tentatively ran his fingers across her breast.

She sighed with obvious pleasure.

It was at that point Steve realized that it was not Jessica who needed protection from him, but it was himself who was in danger of being seduced by the woman who had been driving him insane for the past few weeks.

He quickly unfastened her blouse and slid it from her shoulders with her full cooperation. When Jessica fumbled with his belt buckle, he reached down to stop her, or was it to help her? At this point, he wasn't sure he knew what he was doing and she was being no help at all.

Within minutes Steve had made a pad of sorts of the clothes each of them had been wearing for them to lie on. Before he could consider the wisdom or consequences of what was happening, Jessica was back in his arms, kissing him, stroking him, sliding her leg between his.

She was driving him wild and he could no more resist her than the moon could resist circling the earth. Jessica's gravitational pull for him was every bit as strong.

Steve felt ready to explode by the time she lay beneath him, her quickened breathing and frantic touches eagerly coaxing him to taste, touch, devour.

He lowered his body over her and kissed her deeply at the same time he possessed her body. He paused, waiting for her to adjust to him. She had tightened almost unbearably around him, her legs and arms clamped around him. Then she raised her hips slightly, encouraging him to move.

Steve lost track of space and time as he explored all of the wonders that Jessica offered. She responded to him without inhibition, giving herself totally with no reservation. Never had Steve experienced such trust, so much willingness to be vulnerable with him.

Somehow he had to show her that her trust was not misplaced. He carefully paced himself, encouraging her to experience everything that they shared to the fullest extent.

When he could no longer hang on to his control, he caught her to him and with one final surge buried himself deep within her.

They lay there in the blackness holding each other tightly, trying to get some air in their lungs.

Steve realized that he must have dozed off because he awakened with a sudden jolt, Jessica still held close in his arms. He shifted slightly and she made a soft sound.

"Jessica?"

"Mmm?"

"Are you all right?"

"Cold," she mumbled, pressing closer to him.

Of course she would be cold. Neither one of them were wearing a stitch of clothing. He sat up and felt around, coming up with their jackets and his pants. He draped them over her, then stretched out beside her once again.

"Steve?"

"Yes?"

"Aren't you cold?" Her hand ran across his chest and he quivered.

"I'm all right."

She spread the jackets over him. "We can share," she murmured, holding him close.

Worse things could happen, Steve thought before he drifted off to sleep.

Jessica stirred, feeling a chill. She tried to pull the covers up higher over her shoulders and her blouse slid off her hips.

She opened her eyes with a snap and looked around. The first thing she saw was Steve sprawled next to her, sound asleep. The only thing he wore was a slight smile.

Her eyes widened as the events of the night came back to her with alarming swiftness. What had she done? What had *they* done.

Silly girl. You know exactly what you did and you enjoyed every single minute of it.

A fine time for her conscience to kick in. Where had it been last night when she could have really used it? But would she have listened? Trying to be as honest as she could be with herself, Jessica doubted very much if she would have listened to anyone.

The man so peacefully sleeping beside her held her in a prison of fascination, one that she appeared unable to escape. There was so much more to the man than she had first guessed, despite all the hype her mother gave her. Each time she was around him she discovered new layers of personality and talent and virtues.

Take last night, for example. She fully realized that she had seduced him. She wondered how he was going to behave toward her once he woke up. For that matter, she wasn't at all sure she knew what to say or how to explain the inexplicable. She had been overwhelmed with sensations and feelings. He had been a safe harbor for her when the world seemed to be falling apart.

In the early morning sunlight of a new day Jessica discovered that her feelings had not changed in the least. Regardless of what else happened in her life, Steve would continue to be the one she would seek out for stability and reassurance.

Jessica sat up and slipped on her blouse. Now that she was awake, she wasn't as cold as she was uncomfortable. Peering over the side of the ledge, she looked down into the gully. There was no sign of their being hunted, either by man or beast, for which she was devoutly thankful.

When she turned around she let out a startled cry. Steve had not moved from his relaxed position, but he was watching her through narrowed eyes.

She brushed her hair behind her ear and attempted a rather weak smile.

"Good morning."

"Is it?"

She glanced over her shoulder. "I think so. Looks to be another beautiful day."

He did a thorough visual inventory of her and Jessica could feel herself changing colors. Her blouse, the only item of apparel she wore at the moment, barely covered her hips.

"I was wondering if it would be safe to leave this place?"

He sat up and reached for his pants, pulling them up over his long legs from his seated position. "Safer, probably," he muttered, as though to himself.

Jessica turned away and finished dressing. "What are we going to do now?"

Steve felt the throb of a headache. He thought it interesting that Jessica should voice the very question that had been running through his mind. What in the hell was he supposed to say or do after last night? How had he allowed the situation to get so much out of control?

When he didn't answer she asked, "Do you suppose Mr. Johanson has been looking for us?"

"There's a strong possibility." He crawled to the edge of the cave and studied the surrounding terrain. Then he lowered himself over the side and climbed down.

"Where are you going?"

"Just stay here for a moment. I want to take a look around."

Jessica watched him disappear around the curve of the gully. How could she stay here? She had to go to the bathroom. He couldn't expect her to stay up here waiting for him to show up. With fresh determination she forced herself over the side and carefully found handholds.

Feeling almost as if she were a dauntless explorer Jessica turned the other way from the way Steve went and headed for the blessed cover of the thick foliage to answer nature's call.

She hurried so that he wouldn't know she had not followed his command. There was no need to antagonize the man. After finding a likely spot she quickly took care of her needs and turned back to where she had left the trail. After going a little way, she stopped, looking around. Surely she should have reached the trail. She'd only gone a little way from it. Now there was no sign of it.

Great. She could already hear Steve now, giving her a bad time for getting herself lost.

Lost! The word hit her like a sudden punch in the solar plexus. No, she couldn't be. She started running, hoping to find a clearing so she could look up at the sky. Maybe if she knew where the sun was, she could get an idea of her direction.

When she tripped her hurried pace caused her to fall headlong toward the ground, her nose coming to rest within inches of a hand. A lifeless hand, at the end of a lifeless arm, lay stretched out in front of her.

Jessica screamed, then screamed again, her voice echoing through the bush. She could see the man now, lying on his back with his throat cut.

"Jessica! Jessica, where are you!"

Steve. He was somewhere behind her. She lunged to her feet and started running toward the sound of his voice.

"Steve! Where are you?"

She saw the movement of the low lying brush just before he pushed it aside several yards from her. She covered the ground between them in a couple of leaps and threw herself on him, bringing them both to the ground.

"What the hell! Damn it, Jessica. Have you *ever* done anything that anyone has asked of you in your life? What the hell do you mean, leaving the cave and—"

"S-Steve. I j-ju- I just saw a m-m-man and—"

"What? Where? Where is he?" He fought to get their limbs untangled and came to his feet.

She pointed, unable to say another word. When he started off she grabbed a hold of his hand and he came to an abrupt halt.

"He's dead," she stated in a stark voice.

Shaking her hand off, Steve resumed his search. Within minutes he found the man. There was no doubt but that he was dead. Kneeling, he checked the body. He would guess the man had only been dead for several hours.

He searched for identification but found none. No weapons. Nothing. He'd been stripped clean of identifying marks. There were no labels in his shirt or pants. His boots were well worn.

"Who is he?" Jessica whispered from behind him.

He shook his head, rising.

Steve took her hand and led her away. She followed along behind him, not saying a word. He found a trail that headed in the direction they needed to go and he set a steady pace.

A little more than two hours later they came out on a well-travelled dirt road. Steve paused, looking in both directions. Making a decision, he turned and started following it. Every once in a while he checked on Jessica. She hadn't said anything more since they'd left the body. She was in shock and he knew he had to get her away from here as rapidly as possible.

They came across a small home with a couple of children playing in the front yard.

"Hi. Do you know where Mr. Johanson's place is?"

The older of the two looked at him for a moment in silence, then pointed in the direction they were traveling.

"Thanks."

Steve stopped for a moment and rubbed Jessica's shoulders. She rolled her head in obvious appreciation.

"I don't suppose you could tell me what possessed you to go exploring on your own?" he asked in a gentle voice, his hands continuing to knead her neck muscles.

"I had to go to the bathroom."

He grinned. He got a clear picture of her obvious predicament. Turning her to face him, he enfolded her in his arms.

"I'm sorry I yelled at you, princess. You have no idea how scared I was when I returned and found you gone. I didn't know if whoever had been shooting at us had found you; I didn't know what to think. And then when I heard you scream, my heart gave out on me."

The two children stood watching them with avid curiosity. Steve winked at them, then dropped his arm around Jessica's shoulders and started down the road once again.

They saw the homestead after another mile and Jessica let out a sigh. Steve wasn't sure he felt as relieved but he hoped he could count on Johanson to get them back to Sydney.

Mr. Johanson appeared on the steps and watched them as they walked toward him. "Did you get lost? I warned you about getting lost, didn't I?"

"You certainly did," Steve replied. He helped Jessica up the steps. "Why don't you get a shower and try to rest, okay?" he said to her in a low voice. She nodded without saying anything to Johanson.

As soon as she disappeared inside the house, Steve turned to Johanson. "We ran into a little problem out there."

Johanson's eyes narrowed. "What sort of a problem?"

"Someone shooting at us."

"Are you sure? Maybe it was someone who didn't know you were out there."

"Oh, he knew all right. Quite a marksman, actually."

"Did you see him?"

"No. I decided not to hang around and point out the error of his ways."

Johanson permitted himself a small smile.

"Then this morning we found a body." He described the man and the way he was dressed. Johanson paled. "But I know him." He turned toward the door of the house and called out.

"Frederick, come here."

One of the men who had met them at the airport appeared. "Have you seen Peter this morning?"

"No, sir."

"Find out the last time anyone has seen him."

He turned to Steve. "Peter is one of my gardeners. I can't imagine what he was doing out in the bush in the first place. How was he killed?"

Steve told him in short, succinct sentences. Then he said, "Under the circumstances, I think you can understand that Jessica needs to get back to Sydney. This has been very upsetting to her."

"And to you, as well, I would assume," Johanson said with a steady regard.

"Yes."

"I'm certain your stay out in the wilds overnight could not have been pleasant."

"It was all right. We found a cave to sleep in."

"How resourceful of you."

Steve returned his steady regard. "Brought back the years of scouting I did as a boy."

"Mmm" was the noncommittal reply.

"If you don't mind, I'd like to get cleaned up," Steve went on.

"Certainly. In the meantime, I'll make arrangements to have you flown back to Sydney."

"Thank you. We both appreciate what you've done for us."

While Steve stood under the hot water beating down on him he tried to analyze Johanson's reactions. Was he surprised to see them? Had he expected them to die out in the bush?

When he got out of the shower, he quickly dressed and went downstairs to eat. The housekeeper had prepared two trays. As soon as he had finished eating, he carried Jessica's tray upstairs and tapped on the door. When there was no answer he opened it and looked inside.

She had showered and crawled into bed still wrapped in her bathrobe. Huddled under the covers she looked like a small child sent to bed without understanding why... sad and forlorn... and utterly irresistible.

He set the tray down, then sat down beside her. He leaned over and caressed her cheek.

"Jessica?"

Her eyes blinked open and she stared at him, her alarm apparent.

"It's all right, princess. It's just me. I brought you something to eat. Then you'll need to get dressed. Johanson is sending us back to Sydney."

She sat up and slipped her arms around his waist. He hugged her to him. "I'm sorry about everything that's happened," he said, holding her close. "You shouldn't have had to go through all of this."

"You've been through it, too."

"I know."

Jessica leaned back and looked at him. "Are you sorry about what happened last night?"

"It shouldn't have happened."

"I know. But are you sorry?"

Steve struggled to be honest with her. "No, I'm afraid I can't regret something that I've wanted for a long time."

She smiled at him. "Me, too. I finally decided that since you're determined to be such a gentleman that I'd have to be the one to seduce you."

He leaned down and kissed her cheek, then nuzzled her nose. "You did an excellent job."

"Are you sure? I felt like such an amateur."

"An amateur!" He pulled back and looked at her. "What did you think I expected, a professional?"

She shook her head, running her hand up through his hair. "You know what I mean. It's one thing to read passionate love scenes in all the novels. It's another to actually do what they've described."

He grinned. "All I can say is, you certainly picked up your skills quickly and extremely well."

"Then you weren't disappointed?"

He leaned down and kissed her, taking his time. When he eventually raised his head they were both breathing hard.

"Were you?" he whispered.

She shook her head.

Steve recognized that his disappointment in what had happened was the timing, not the event. He wanted more than one night of shared anxiety over their situation. He wanted the opportunity to love her, to kiss and caress her, to be able to see her enjoyment of what they shared.

Hopefully, there would be other times. First, he needed to get her back to some sort of safety. He needed to contact Max, and he needed to find Trevor Randall.

Whatever was going on around Eric Johanson needed to be investigated, as well. There were too many other urgent priorities for him at the moment. Once they were resolved he and Jessica would need to sit down and talk about their relationship.

The one thing he wouldn't allow her to ignore was the fact that they had, indeed, established a relationship. He intended to let her know that he wanted to make it permanent, no matter what adjustments they needed to make in their lives.

But not now. There was no time now. He had to make sure that she was safe.

Ten

———

I've got some more info on Eric Johanson," Max said as soon as Steve identified himself.

"Let's hear it."

"Eric Johanson came into being about twenty years ago, about the time Edwin Randall moved from England to Australia and disappeared without a trace."

"Randall?"

"That's right. Eric Johanson is Trevor Randall's older brother."

"Damn, then he must be aware of my investigation."

"At least the early stages when you were first following up on some of your leads for the other story in England."

"Why didn't this information turn up in your first report?"

"It seems that Edwin and Trevor have friends in very high places on both continents."

"Uh-oh. I take it we're treading on some delicate toes these days."

"You know how pushy those dratted Americans are," Max drawled.

"What was the reason for the name change?"

"He was making it clear that he had no use for the entire family, Trevor included, and in fact has never returned, even when his elderly mother died a few years after he left."

"Johanson, or whoever you want to call him, must be in his seventies. Why wait until he's in his fifties to immigrate and change his name?"

"Perhaps you could ask him. It didn't turn up. The person we finally coaxed to give us the information was a close friend of the family for many years. She explained how heartbroken the mother was when her son moved away and commented on how glad she was that her dear friend didn't live to know of the gruesome death of the younger son."

"She's talking about Trevor, I take it."

"Yes, she felt quite sure that had he not died, Trevor would have been able to clear up the situation and not leave a dark cloud, as she called it, over the family's good name."

"Then it was no good asking if the brothers got along, I don't suppose," Steve said.

"From all accounts, they never did have much to do with each other because of the gap in their ages. Edwin was a teenager when Trevor appeared on the scene."

"But if Trevor wanted to disappear, it seems logical that he might contact his brother whose name was no longer the same as his."

"Could be."

"What I don't understand is why Edwin/Eric called my attention to him in the first place."

"You underestimate your skills and your reputation as a reporter. He must have decided to wield his power and have a close up view of the man who might be looking for his brother."

"Maybe."

"I doubt that he has any idea of your other work."

"I wouldn't swear to that. Someone tried to kill both of us yesterday while Jessica and I were out exploring the countryside."

"How?"

"Rifle. Excellent eye, I might add."

"Were either of you hurt?"

"No, but the next morning we stumbled on to the body of a man who Johanson later claimed to be one of his gardeners by the name of Peter."

"Any last name?"

"I didn't feel it politic to suggest he tell me, under the circumstances. I'm already fully apprised of his opinion regarding reporters."

"Do you think he was behind the shooting?"

"I wouldn't hazard a guess, at this point. What I need to know from you is whether to pursue the investigation about Randall. Do you want me to find him, see what he says, get an interview, what? Somehow I sense that a man who faked his own death isn't going to be too forthcoming about sharing his new life with others.''

"If you could locate and positively identify him, we'd then be in a position to turn over our information to the British authorities to take whatever action they deem necessary. At this point we don't have a positive ID on the man, just conjecture and someone who says he may have seen a man who resembles the picture we have of Trevor Randall.''

Steve sighed. "All right. I'll see what I can do.''

"In the meantime, find out what you can about the dead gardener. Maybe he knew too much and your host got nervous.''

"All right.''

"What about Jessica? What do you intend to do about her?''

"Send her back to the States, if she'll go.''

"Can't you just tell her to go?''

"Of course I can. And nothing would create a stronger determination for her to stay than for me to suggest that I think she should leave.''

"Obstinate?''

"The word could have been created with her in mind.''

"Surely she understands the danger after the shooting incident.''

"I think I managed to convince her it was an isolated incident.''

"And she bought your theory?''

"No. She thinks I'm naïve.''

"Naïve!''

"Yes. She thinks that Johanson is a drug smuggler, afraid I'm going to do a television exposé on him and he's trying to frighten me."

"Drug smuggler?"

"Yeah."

"In Australia?"

"Yeah."

"Hmm."

"She thinks the dead gardener was trying to warn us not to go back to the house, when whoever was shooting at us spotted him and killed him."

"I see."

"Jessica thinks that if I confront Johanson with the power of the news media, that he will crumble in fear and admit everything to me."

"My God. Where did she get such ideas?"

"A combination of what's been playing on the six o'clock news mixed in with drama on television. Oh, and she also thinks I'm either a drug or arms smuggler or a mercenary."

Max made a sound that Steve couldn't interpret. After a moment, Steve asked, "You still there?"

"Uh, yes. I, uh, was left speechless there for a moment."

"Thought you might be."

"Good luck on attempting to get her to return to the States."

"Glad you can see my problem."

When they hung up Steve began to pace around the small room. He didn't know what to do about Jessica. She'd been talking about visiting Melbourne and possibly Adelaide by the time they reached her hotel.

Thoughts of being shot at and stumbling over dead bodies seemed to have been pushed to the back of her mind.

Steve sincerely hoped so, while at the same time he wished he could be certain that she hadn't been the prime target. After all, the first shot was aimed at her, not him. That had bothered him ever since it happened.

Could someone think Jessica was mixed up in his investigation just because they were together? If they wanted to stop him, why get her? Unless they intended to make it clear to him they meant business. Perhaps they thought he might back off for her sake, where he wouldn't necessarily do so if threats were made to him.

Steve came to a stop in the middle of the room. If his supposition was correct, all they would have to do was to go after her now. She was alone and defenseless.

He spun on his heel and grabbed the phone. Quickly dialing the hotel number, he waited impatiently for them to answer. When they did, he asked for her room number.

"Are you calling for Ms. Sheldon?"

"Yes."

"I don't believe she's in her room at the moment, sir. You see, the police had some questions and they—"

"The police! What's wrong? What happened?"

"I really couldn't say, sir, other than she rang down about half an hour ago and requested that I call the police, which I did."

"Where is she now?"

"I believe they requested that she accompany them to the station."

"Omigod."

Steve hung up the phone and stared at it feeling something close to horror. Then he called his local contact and explained the situation. He was told to sit tight and someone would get back to him and let him know where Jessica had been taken.

Within minutes the phone rang and Steve was given the address where he could find her. He lost no time in getting there.

He was running up the steps when he saw Jessica come out the door, chatting with a uniformed policeman. When she saw Steve she said, "Oh, here's Steve now. He'll give me a lift back to my hotel. Thank you for offering." Then she trotted down the stairs. "How did you know where to find me? I tried to call you but—"

He grabbed her arm and started toward the car. "You tried to call me when?"

"I don't know the time, but the line was busy and I was afraid the guy would come to before I could decide what to do about him, which is exactly what happened by the way, so that by the time the police got there he was gone," she said with disgust.

"What guy? What happened? Were you hurt?"

"Do I look hurt? What's wrong with you, anyway? You're shaking."

Steve finally noticed that the reason he was having difficulty getting the key in the ignition switch was because his hand was trembling. He fought to gain some control before he said, "I tell you what, Jessica. Why don't we take a nice, leisurely ride back over to the hotel, enjoy the sights along the way and just not talk for a while. Then, after we get to the hotel and your room, maybe we'll both be in the mood to discuss—" his voice had become increasingly louder until he finished with "—what in the hell happened!"

Jessica folded her hands in her lap and looked out the window without responding.

Steve jabbed the key into the ignition and started the car. True to his word he didn't open his mouth until they had parked the car, gone into the hotel, crossed the lobby, waited for the elevator, rode the elevator to her floor, walked to her door, unlocked it and went inside.

He sat down in the chair beside the window, looked at her and said, "Please start at the beginning."

"The beginning of what?"

"Of whatever happened today."

Jessica sat down on the bed immediately across from him and looked down at her hands. "I don't understand why you're angry."

"Somehow that doesn't surprise me."

She sighed. "All right. I had decided to go shopping today—" She paused and looked at him with an expression of eagerness. "Do you want to see what I found? It is absolutely—"

"Later. What happened when you got back to the room?"

"I opened the door and as I walked past the bathroom this guy suddenly stepped out."

His heart sank. "Go on."

In a defensive voice, she said, "Well, he scared me."

"I can imagine."

"I wasn't expecting anyone to be here and when he appeared like that I responded by reflex."

"Meaning?"

"I, uh, used my martial arts training and somehow, when he fell, he hit his head on the dresser and knocked himself out."

"I see. Your martial arts training," he repeated carefully.

"I learned some basic moves at a self-defense class I took right after I moved to Manhattan. I mean, you hear so many stories about what can happen that I thought I'd feel safer if I knew how to protect myself."

"Uh-huh."

"It really scared me because I thought at first he was dead. You can't imagine my relief when I saw he was breathing."

"Mmm."

"I wasn't sure what to do, so I called you but you were on the phone for so long I finally got tired of dialing. That's when I thought about calling the police. The man down at the desk was kind enough to make the call for me."

"Yes. He told me."

"Oh, so that's how you knew about what happened."

"Why did you leave with the police?"

"Because they wanted to know if I could identify him and I told them I could if I could see a picture of him. So they had me go down with them—"

"—and look at mug shots."

"Right."

"Oh, Jessica."

"Steve, why are you looking at me like that? What did I do wrong?"

He shook his head. "You did nothing wrong. You just continue to surprise me, that's all. Were you able to identify him?"

"Not really. They look so different in those pictures. I gave them a general description of him, though."

Steve leaned forward and buried his head in his hands. Jessica went down on her knees in front of him and put her arms around his neck. "Please tell me what's wrong."

He put his arms around her and held her to him. "Oh, Jessica, what am I going to do about you?"

"Do you think this had anything to do with what happened up in Queensland?"

"To be truthful, yes, I do. I believe that someone is trying to control me through you and they're doing a damned good job of it, I have to admit."

"But why?"

"They want me to stop my investigation."

"Or else?"

"Something like that."

"But you're not going to let that stop you, are you?"

"Jessica, I can't think when you're here, don't you know that? You've got me tied in knots." He touched his lips to hers. "I want you to go back to New York, where the only thing you have to worry about are muggers. I need to be free of worry about you.''

"You don't think I can take care of myself?''

"I know you can. You've proved that. But that bullet came too close. You can't protect yourself from something like that. You wouldn't have had a chance if the intruder in your room had been holding a gun. He would have nailed you as you came through the door.''

Jessica leaned into Steve, holding him close as she knelt there on the floor in front of him. "If that's what you want, I'll leave. Between my interview with Gregory and my notes from Mr. Johanson, I think I can write an article that will successfully promote tourism in Australia.''

He cupped her face in his hands. "I'm sorry all of this has worked out this way. You would have been much better off coming to Australia alone.''

"Don't say that. I'm glad I came with you, Steve. I don't regret a thing that's happened. You are so very special to me.'' She touched his lips with her fingers and he kissed them. She traced the shape of his brow, the line of his jaw.

"Jessica?''

Her gaze met his. "Yes?''

"I want to make love to you.''

She could feel her love for him swell within her, growing ever larger. There was no arrogance now. Just need . . . and vulnerability.

"I'd like that very much,'' she whispered.

As he rose from the chair he brought her up with him. She stood before him, waiting. He had never seen

so much trust in her eyes before. He could feel his
body trembling with the urgent need to claim her, to
become a part of her. He reached for her and she
flowed into his arms as though she knew that was
where she belonged.

He unzipped the back of her dress, then slid it from
her shoulders. The rest of her clothes soon followed.

Jessica remained before him unashamed and Steve
knew in that moment that this woman was his as truly
as if God had placed her in his arms. Whatever the
circumstances that had brought them together, their
coming together was inevitable.

He quickly discarded his clothes and led her to the
bed. He guided her to its surface, then followed her.
His kisses blazed a trail of discovery as he explored
every inch of her, touching and tasting her with each
tiny kiss.

Her skin glowed, its satiny smoothness coaxing him
to stroke her until she reached for him.

"Don't tease me, Steve. Please, not now."

"If anyone is being teased, princess, it's me." His
lips found the tip of her breast and he ran his tongue
over the taut surface.

She reached for him and at her touch, he groaned.
He rolled so that she was beneath him. Nudging her
legs apart he knelt between them, slowly lowering
himself until he filled her completely.

"Oh, Steve."

"Am I hurting you?"

"Oh, no. Never."

His patience gone, Steve began a rhythm that
quickly lifted them both away from their surround-

ings. He held her tightly as she seemed to explode with inner contractions, her soft cries encouraging him to continue loving her until, with one last convulsive lunge, he felt as though he, too, exploded, losing all sense of identity that didn't include the woman who held him so strongly in her arms.

Steve remained with her through the night, loving her again and again, storing up memories for the time when they would no longer be together.

Eleven

Jessica heard the phone ringing when she reached the top of the stairs of her floor. She fumbled for the key, shifting the two sacks of groceries she carried.

"Wait a minute. I'll be there as soon as I can."

Every time the phone rang, at home or at work, her heart jumped in her chest, wondering if it would be Steve. At the moment that same organ was leaping around from the combination of climbing the stairs and wondering if she would get to the phone before whoever was calling hung up.

Forcing her hand to remain steady, Jessica jammed the key into the lock and twisted, pushing against the door at the same time. As the dead bolt unlocked, she grabbed the doorknob, turned it, and almost fell as her weight against the door propelled her into the room when it swung open. She used her momentum to get across the room and set the groceries on the counter.

Grabbing the phone, she said, "H'lo!"

"Jessica?"

Jessica took a deep breath and tried to make her heart stop jumping around like a frog in her chest. "Oh, hi, Mom."

"I didn't recognize you, honey. Is something wrong?"

"I just got home. I was on the landing when I heard the phone, so I'm a little out of breath."

"Since I hadn't heard from you in the last two weeks, I thought I'd see how you were doing."

"I've been busy. My desk was covered with work with short deadlines when I returned to the office."

"You'll need a vacation just to rest up from being gone."

"Probably. So how are the twins? And Michael?"

Jessica sank onto the chair by the phone and listened as her mother told her about all the family activities since they had last spoken. Jessica had called home as soon as she returned to New York to let them know of her arrival. She had mailed them the gifts she had found for them and Sabrina told her how much they had enjoyed them. Jessica had received carefully printed notes from each of the twins thanking her. Now she heard about what they had said when they opened their packages and what they had done with the toys and clothing she'd found for them.

When Sabrina paused Jessica forced herself to sound casual as she asked, "Heard anything from Steve?"

"No, but then we rarely do. You know how he is. Hates to write and rarely calls. He's probably back to work by now, don't you imagine?"

"I have no idea. Remember I never tried to keep up with him."

"No," her mother drawled, "and you used to never ask about him, either. Is it possible you're softening a little toward the man?"

"Oh, Mother, don't be ridiculous. I was just wondering if he was still in Australia, that's all." She hadn't told anyone about what had happened to her and Steve while they were together. There was no reason to upset her mother, but Jessica knew that the events she and Steve had shared had made such an impact on her life that nothing, for her, would ever be quite the same again.

"Well, I'm pleased that at least the two of you have gotten a little better acquainted. You're family, after all."

"I know, Mom."

How ironic. All those years she'd been forced to listen to her mother go on and on about Steve. Now, when she yearned to hear any tidbit of information about him, her mother knew nothing.

"I really need to get my groceries put away, Mom. Tell everyone hello for me and tell the twins I enjoyed their thank-you notes very much. I'm extremely impressed."

Sabrina laughed. "You should be. I don't want to tell you the hours they labored over those things."

When Jessica hung up the phone she put her groceries away, made a small salad and heated up a can of soup. When she sat down to eat it, her thoughts drifted back to her last evening in Australia.

Even though she'd agreed to leave, it took some rescheduling of her airline ticket to get her on a flight back to San Francisco. She was unable to leave the day after Steve asked her to go, but was booked for the second day. Steve never left her side until she was about to board the plane.

She would never forget that day and night. They had taken a ferry ride across Sydney Harbour, explored the shops, had a drink at Argyle Tavern. In short, they did all of the tourist-type things that a visitor would do in Sydney.

Steve had made reservations for dinner at one of the restaurants overlooking the city and the Harbour. They had stopped by his apartment for him to change and while they were there his landlord stopped by to apologize for having gone into his apartment a few days before. Someone had reported a leak and he had come in to check the plumbing in Steve's bathroom. She noticed that Steve had a strange look on his face at the explanation, but he never offered a reason and she didn't feel comfortable asking. Had Steve known someone had come in? If so, she wondered how he would be able to detect such a thing.

Steve had turned out to be an enigma, but one she continued to find fascinating. He had hidden skills that continued to surprise her whenever they surfaced. Where she had thought him to be arrogant and boastful, she now saw that she couldn't have been further from the truth.

She smiled when she remembered their return to her hotel to dress that final evening.

The tension had grown steadily between them as the day progressed. Every time he looked at her, every time he touched her, she thought she was going to burst into flames.

He unlocked the door and walked in first, making sure there were no surprises awaiting them. Then he motioned for her to come inside. She no sooner closed the door and turned back to him than he had his arms around her, kissing her.

This was what she had wanted all day, to be able to touch him, to hold him close, to experience the magic of his lovemaking again.

They both seemed to explode with passion. She didn't remember how they had managed to remove their clothes. All she recalled was being on the bed with him while his kisses turned her into molten lava, flowing over and around him.

Sitting there in her small apartment Jessica could still recall the way his hands had gently explored her body, the way his lips had caressed her breasts, the way his fingers had found her most sensitive spot and lovingly stroked her until she could stand no more.

She'd begged Steve to come to her and he had needed no further encouragement, joining their bodies into a perfect oneness. She had clung to him, overwhelmed with all that she was feeling, wanting the moment to go on and on and on....

Later they had showered together, laughing and teasing, soaping and rinsing, then carefully drying each other until their desire had steadily grown once more.

"We've got to get dressed or we're going to miss our reservations," Steve whispered after several heated kisses.

"All right," she managed to say, pulling away from him.

They dressed and arrived in time to be seated at a small table for two before a wide expanse of glass that gave them an unimpeded view of the Harbour at night.

A large candle shed light on the table, creating an island of intimacy for them...candlelight for two. Jessica would never forget how the soft light emphasized the quiet strength of Steve's face—the high cheekbones, strong jawline—glinting off his dark hair.

He reached for her hand. "Do you have any idea how beautiful you are?" he asked.

"I was thinking the same thing about you."

He quirked an eyebrow.

"Well, handsome, then."

"I'm not sure I agree with that one, but I'm feeling too mellow to argue with you tonight."

Jessica grinned. "That's a first."

"We do seem to get into some heated discussions, from time to time. I wonder why?"

"Because we're both highly opinionated individuals, perhaps?"

"Perhaps. I must admit that you keep me on my toes, trying to stay ahead of you."

"And do you find it necessary to stay ahead?"

His smile made her insides melt. "I don't think I'll ever manage that feat, anyway. It's all I can do to stay up with you and several times I haven't managed that. You never cease to surprise me."

"How?"

"About the time I think I understand you, you do or say something that opens up a whole new facet of your personality I never knew existed."

"That accurately describes the way I feel with you. I never know what to expect. Take that pistol, for instance. You handle it like a professional."

Steve started to say something, then paused. He reached for his glass of wine, as though needing a moment to think. When he replaced the glass on the table, he seemed to have made up his mind about something.

"That's because I am, princess."

"You are what?" she asked, puzzled by the serious expression he wore.

"A professional."

Jessica studied him for a moment. "I don't think I understand."

"In my senior year at college I was recruited to work as a covert agent for a little known agency of our government. In addition to my chosen career, I agreed to work as much as possible to gather information to help keep track of what was happening around the world."

She stared at him. "Like a spy?"

"Well, I don't go skulking down dark alleyways wearing a trench coat." He thought about that for a minute. "Yet," he finally added.

"Is that why you're over here now?"

"Yes."

"So whoever shot at us may already know that."

"That's what I'm afraid of. It may be a coincidence, but I don't want to count on it and take that chance, because of you. You mean a great deal to me, you must know that by now."

Jessica smiled, and she knew Steve must be able to see her feelings for him radiating from her. "I was beginning to gather that," she said, her smile spreading into a mischievous grin.

Steve's expression sobered. "What has happened between us was totally unexpected for me."

"Me, too."

"There's so much at stake, for both of us. I don't want to rush into anything that might create a painful situation where the family's concerned."

"Steve... I would never ask anything of you that you weren't comfortable with or willing to give to me. Please understand that."

Their dinner arrived, and by unspoken mutual consent, the conversation turned away from personal subjects.

Jessica's thoughts returned to the present. She washed the dishes she'd used and went into the bathroom. A long hot soak in the tub might help her relax. She couldn't keep her mind off the last day she and Steve had spent together. How many times had she reflected on it, reliving each moment, particularly when they had returned to her hotel room. Steve had purchased another bottle of wine, and she realized that, like her, Steve wanted to prolong their evening as much as possible.

They intended to sit and watch the Harbour from her window, seeing the lights of the ferries as they skimmed across the black surface, but all they had been able to do was to look at each other. Looking soon wasn't enough and they had touched, kissed and caressed until they had ended up in bed once more.

Later they had propped themselves up in bed, sipped the wine and shared their most intimate thoughts.

Steve told her what it had been like, at the age of ten, to have been moved so far away from the father whom he'd adored. The resultant pain had never quite gone away.

Jessica shared something she had never told another living soul. Jessica's grandmother on her father's side had died when Jessica was fifteen. And at that time, a member of the family had shipped the few mementos her grandmother still had of Jessica's father to her.

Sabrina had saved pictures for her, but these were trophies her father had won in sports, athletic letters, certificates and yearbooks, both high school and college.

She'd gone through everything, trying to feel something for the man she couldn't remember. She'd been looking through his college yearbook when she came across a letter that had been written to him less than a month before he was killed in a racing car accident. It was written on school notebook paper and looked similar to the notes she used to pass to her girlfriends when she was in school.

The note was signed by someone named Kathy and from what had been written, Jessica realized that her father had been involved with Kathy. The unknown woman's comments were obviously in response to things her father had said to her. Kathy talked about their future plans after he was free.

Jessica would never forget her shock and her disillusionment. She determined then and there that her mother would never know that the man she'd loved so much that she had waited over sixteen years after his death to remarry, had so quickly forgotten his commitment to her. Her parents had only been married three years when her father died.

Jessica admitted to Steve that discovering her father's unfaithfulness at such a vulnerable age had colored her attitude toward all men. She'd never had a close relationship with a man because she couldn't bring herself to trust one.

She would never forget Steve's sympathy and understanding as she had shared her pain with him. The amazing thing was how much lighter she felt after having told him. Her feelings about men in general were too involved with her unexpected knowledge about her father for her to be able to sit down and discuss some of her fears with her mother, so she had kept them to herself and allowed her fear of relationships to grow. Until now—her feelings for Steve had jolted her into confessing and admitting her anxieties and her inability to get close to a man.

Somehow Jessica must have known from the time she first met him that Steve had the ability to break through the barriers she had placed around herself, which was probably why she had been so antagonistic toward him whenever he was around. He was a threat to her comfortable existence.

Lying in bed with Steve, having him hold her close, having him be open with her and share his past hurts, had broken down all of her walls. They had talked long into the night, then had fallen silent as they expressed what they were sharing in a more physical way. This time the passion that kept drawing them together was absent.

Their lovemaking became a healing, at least for her, Jessica knew. Steve's gentleness with her, his consideration and concern for her pleasure made her heart take wing.

She loved Steve Donovan with all of her heart. She knew that without any doubt. But she was not going to allow her love for him to build expectations of a future with him.

They never discussed the possibility of a future. Perhaps they would never have again what they shared while they were in Australia. She could accept that if she must.

Steve told her that he would call and let her know what happened once she left and Jessica knew that he would do that, eventually. For the first time she was truly grateful for the family tie that enabled her to stay in touch with him, if no more than through their respective parents.

He had taught her so much about herself. She had been living her life at twenty-five by the rules she had made up at fifteen. Steve had helped her to see that she no longer needed to do that....

Jessica realized that her bath water had grown cold while she'd been sitting there thinking about Steve. She climbed out of the tub and rubbed herself dry with one of the large bath towels Sabrina had sent her as a housewarming gift when she moved into her apartment.

She looked at the clock. It was after eight o'clock. Too early for bed but she wasn't in the mood to go out. One of the women at work had suggested they get a bite to eat and catch a movie, but she'd begged off, not wanting to admit that she didn't want to take the chance of missing Steve's call.

She had to stop planning her time around the phone. She knew that, but somehow nothing else seemed to be as important as the possibility of hearing from Steve. She had it bad and she knew it.

Jessica put on one of her favorite instrumental tapes and found a book to read. The book was engrossing enough that she forgot the time, forgot everything but the story that she followed.

When the knock sounded at her door she jerked and almost screamed. Automatically she glanced at the clock. It was after ten. Who would be knocking at that time of the night? She didn't know any of her neighbors.

She checked the lock and peered through her security hole. She couldn't believe it. Hastily she unfastened the chain and lock and opened the door.

"Steve! What are you doing here! Come in." Jessica stepped back and allowed him to step inside.

He looked haggard, as though he hadn't slept in days. He hadn't shaved in a while and his clothes were wrinkled.

He looked wonderful to her. She threw her arms around him. "It's so good to see you. But what are you doing in New York City?"

Steve picked her up and carried her to her overstuffed armchair and sat down with her in his lap. He held Jessica against him without saying anything, as though he were receiving some life-giving sustenance by the act.

Questions ran around in Jessica's head but she realized that none of them were as important as holding him, as knowing that he had come to her, was there now with her.

She became aware that she was in her poor, bedraggled bathrobe, the one that was stained and had a button missing. But it didn't matter. Nothing mattered but Steve.

She rested her head on his shoulder and waited.

After several minutes of silence, Steve sighed and said, "You don't know how much I needed to do that."

She smiled and touched his cheek. It felt rough to her sensitive fingers.

"I don't remember the last time I shaved," he muttered.

"It doesn't matter. I'm so glad you're here."

"I didn't intend to come here. I should be in London right now. But when it came time to fly out of Sydney, I couldn't force myself on that plane. I had to see you. I've missed you so damned much."

His hands hadn't been idle while he spoke. He touched her face, her neck, her shoulders. His other hand kept tracing the same path along her thigh and hip as though reassuring himself that she was real.

"You look so tired."

He laid his head on the back of the chair and sighed, closing his eyes. "I am."

"Are you through with your assignment?"

"Yes."

"Can you talk about it?"

He smiled. "I suppose I can, but right now I'm too tired to think straight."

"When was the last time you ate?"

He rolled his head across the back of the chair. "On the plane, I think."

"Let me make you something to eat while you go shower, okay?"

He yawned. "All right."

Jessica wiggled off his lap, then turned and reached for his hand. "Are you going to need help?" she teased.

He opened his eyes and she was stunned by the look of love he gave her. "I might."

Steve stood and she led the way into her bedroom. She went into the bathroom and found him a towel and washcloth, then came out of the small room.

"There you are. I'll have something ready when you're through."

She busied herself by quickly making some sandwiches and filled a small bowl with some of the salad she'd made earlier. She also made some coffee.

Jessica heard the shower turn off and when he didn't come out of the bedroom in a few minutes, she decided to see if he needed something. She paused in the doorway between the living area and the bedroom. In the dim light Jessica saw that Steve had come out of the bathroom with a towel wrapped around his waist and had stretched out across the bed.

He was sound asleep.

Twelve

Jessica walked back into the kitchen, covered the sandwiches and placed them in the refrigerator, returned the salad to the larger container and poured the coffee into a thermos.

She returned to the bedroom and looked at Steve for a moment. He had flown halfway around the world to be with her. She had no way of knowing what had been happening in his life for the last two weeks, but she had a suspicion that he hadn't been getting much rest.

The important thing was that he had come to her. She moved to the bed and started to pull the covers down.

"Steve."

There was no response.

"Why don't you get into bed? You'll rest more comfortably...and so will I." Otherwise she wouldn't have a place to sleep. He had managed to take up the whole bed.

He didn't move. Jessica leaned over and rubbed his shoulder. "Steve?"

He sighed and rubbed his cheek into the bedspread.

"Please move over."

Steve lifted his head and looked at her, his eyes unfocused. She lifted the covers. "Why don't you get under these?"

He sat up and looked around as though trying to figure out where he was. Without a word he followed her suggestion and slid between the sheets, losing his towel in the process.

Jessica found a gown to sleep in, slipped off her robe and pulled the nightgown over her head, then turned out the light and crawled into bed with Steve.

She curled up to his back, loving the long length of him; his warmth, the feel of his hair-roughened legs against hers. She had no idea what would happen tomorrow. She didn't care.

Sometime in the night Jessica roused enough to remember that Steve was there. This time he was curled around her, his arm across her waist, hugging her to him, one leg thrown over hers. She smiled to herself and drifted off to sleep once more.

Toward dawn Steve jerked awake, his heart pounding. Where was he? How had he allowed himself to fall asleep? He knew better than to fall asleep. He had to—

He suddenly realized there was someone in bed with

him. A faint light came through a window nearby and he raised his head, peering at the woman he clutched to his chest.

Jessica!

The sense of relief that swept over Steve made him weak. Now he remembered. He'd managed to find his way to her. He'd finished his assignment and turned over the details of his investigation to Max, who had contacted the necessary authorities.

And he'd found Trevor Randall.

Someday he might do a story on Trevor, but he didn't believe it would be in the near future. At least Steve had solved some of the riddles that had plagued him during his investigation.

Now all he had to do was to return to London and pick up the details of his life there. As far as the network was concerned, he had been on extended vacation. If he gathered any additional information on the story he'd been working on, they would expect him to use them.

He would have to decide how to handle that part of his job later.

In the meantime, he was now with Jessica. She felt so good in his arms, he wasn't sure that he ever wanted to leave her. He also knew that he had no other choice.

Propping himself on his elbow, Steve looked down at Jessica. She looked so peaceful he hated to wake her. He also knew that there was no way he was going to leave her alone.

He leaned down and kissed her beneath her ear. She stirred slightly and smiled. Considering her response enough encouragement to continue, Steve shifted slightly and edged her over onto her back. His knee slipped between her legs.

He began to place kisses with a delicate touch across her cheek, the sides of her mouth, across her brow, along her neck. Jessica murmured something indistinct and slid her arms around his shoulders.

When he finally found her mouth with his, she accepted his kiss with a sleepy enthusiasm that caused his heart to race. He slipped the straps of her short gown off her shoulders and pulled the gown down to her waist, exposing her breasts. He took his time kissing and caressing each one.

She sighed, moving restlessly.

"Steve?" she whispered, still more than half-asleep.

He chuckled. "I should certainly hope so. Who else were you expecting?"

"I'm so glad you're here," she murmured.

"So am I, princess, believe me."

He continued to kiss and stroke, wanting to touch every inch of her body. His fingers brushed across her inner thigh and Jessica shifted. He wanted her too badly to tease her. Steve shifted, moving over her, her eager entreaties swirling around them.

When he joined them, they both sighed their pleasure. Once again he sought out her mouth, possessing her with rhythmic thrusts of his tongue and body.

He felt her response deep within, her body convulsively clinging to him, causing him to lose any remaining control he had. He clasped her to him, wishing he could freeze the moment so that he never had to let her go.

Later they lay there on the bed, trying to get their breath, their bodies still intimately entwined.

"Welcome home, sailor," Jessica murmured a few minutes later when her breathing had eased.

He chuckled. "What a greeting."

"Are you hungry?"

"Not any more."

"I meant for food, silly."

"Oh, no, I'm all right." He glanced over at the clock. "It's only a little after five. What time do you have to get up?"

"I don't. It's Saturday."

"It's been Friday for two days for me."

"I know. It was weird to leave Sydney at two in the afternoon and arrive in San Francisco at ten o'clock in the morning of the same day."

"Did you have plans for today?"

"Nothing other than routine things."

"Then I haven't interfered with anything?"

"You could never do that, Steve."

She enjoyed the feel of his body still wrapped securely around her. The sensation was something that she could easily become addicted to.

Jessica drifted off to sleep once again.

The ringing of the telephone brought her out of a deep sleep several hours later. She felt so weighed down she could scarcely move. She opened her eyes and realized that Steve was draped over her. She stretched and finally caught the phone by the tips of her fingers.

"H'lo?" she said softly, trying not to disturb Steve.

"Oh, dear," Sabrina said, "I didn't mean to wake you up. I thought for sure you'd be awake by now. Isn't it ten o'clock there?"

Jessica stiffened as though the phone came fully equipped with a television screen, as though her mother could see her in bed with Steve.

"Uh, hi, Mom. I just felt like sleeping in this morning. Is there something wrong at home?"

"Oh, no, I just forgot to tell you when I called yesterday there's a special on cable television tonight about Australia. I thought you might want to watch it."

"Thank you for letting me know."

"Jessica, honey, are you feeling all right? You don't sound like yourself."

She almost groaned aloud. All she wanted to do was to get off the phone before she woke up Steve or gave her mother reason to believe there was anyone with her.

"I'm fine, Mom. Just fine. It's just that I'm not fully awake and—"

As though the world around her moved in slow motion, Jessica watched as Steve slowly drew his arm away from her breast and plucked the receiver out of her hand. She jerked her head around to see what he was doing in time to receive a jolt that took her breath away.

He put the phone against his ear and said, "Good morning, Sabrina. How are things at the lake?"

Jessica slid down and pulled the covers over her head.

The pause after he spoke became a lengthy silence before Sabrina finally made a sound.

In a tentative, bewildered voice, she asked, "Steve?"

"Yes."

"What are you doing at Jessica's?"

He grinned at the shocked reproach he heard in her voice. "Well, as you've probably guessed, we were trying to sleep." He heard a groan from beneath the covers. He patted the mound of covers beside him reassuringly.

"But I thought you were in Australia?"

"I was. I flew straight through to New York. Got in late last night."

There was another long pause, as though Sabrina was searching for something to say.

"How's Dad?"

"Oh, he's fine. He's gone to the lumberyard to get some supplies right now. He wants to do some repair work to the dock. The twins went with him otherwise I'm sure they would all like to talk to you."

"That's all right. I'll give you a call later today."

"How long are you going to be in New York?"

"I'll have to leave tomorrow, I'm afraid."

"Oh."

"You sound surprised to find me here."

"You could say that."

"Didn't Jessica tell you about us?"

Another groan emanated from beneath the covers.

"I'm getting the distinct impression that Jessica left a great deal out of her description of her trip to Australia."

"Oh, well, we can always fill you in on all the details later."

"I take it the two of you are getting along better than you were when you first left here," Sabrina said drily.

Steve laughed. "You could say that. I'm hoping to convince her that she's compromised my reputation and will have to come up with some compensation for her scandalous behavior."

Jessica threw back the covers and glared at him. He gave her his most brilliant smile.

"Would you care to explain that a little, Steve? What exactly has Jessica done?"

"Distracted me, intrigued me, shaken me, infuriated me, captivated me. You name it. She's done it." He rubbed her cheek with his forefinger.

Jessica stared at him with astonishment.

"So," Steve went on, "I decided to come to New York so that we could come up with a workable solution to my dilemma."

Sabrina chuckled. "Sorry for the interruption."

"No problem. Did you want to say anything more to Jessica?"

Jessica frantically shook her head.

"Not at the moment, Steve," Sabrina said. "I'm certain that you have everything under control."

"Thanks for the vote of confidence."

"Oh, and Steve, I'll be sure to let your Dad know that we talked. You know how protective he is of Jessica. He might want to chat with you about your intentions."

Steve laughed. "Tell him that they are pure, absolutely pure."

"Give Jessica my love."

"I'd be delighted. I'll talk to you soon."

"You may be sure of that!"

Steve was still laughing when he hung up the phone. Jessica glared at him. "Would you care to explain what was so funny?"

"Your mother and her sense of humor."

"I think your sense of humor is definitely warped. What do you mean letting her know you were here with me?"

He lifted a brow. "Why? Are you ashamed of me?"

"You know it's not that."

"I don't know anything about what's going on in that mind of yours."

She smiled sweetly. "You mean my quirky mind."

"Precisely. Didn't you tell your mother anything about our time together in Australia?"

"I'm not sure what you expected me to say. 'Oh, by the way, Mom, Steve and I slept together the first night we arrived in Australia. Then, a few days later, we got shot at and had to hide in a cave. We did a lot more that night than sleep!'"

He grinned at her, irritating her further. "I thought you and your mother were close."

"We are. But we don't make a habit of discussing our sex lives!"

"Oh. Does that mean this is the first thing you've managed to keep from your mother?"

"Are you implying that my inexperience is so obvious? I must apologize if I've bored you with my lack of knowledge."

He lunged, grabbing her around the waist, then falling back to the bed, where she sprawled across him. "No. You have not bored me and don't confuse innocence with inexperience. Your innocence has been delightful, but you're a quick study, princess. Your natural instincts are fantastic."

He started kissing her. When she struggled, he just held her to him tighter until she stopped squirming. After a moment she relaxed and wrapped her arms around him, kissing him back.

Steve discovered the perfect distraction for the times when Jessica insisted on arguing with him. He would have to make a list of provocative subjects for the future.

Much, much later Jessica made a large breakfast and they sat in her small kitchen and ate. After Steve cleaned his plate and Jessica refilled his cup of coffee several times she asked, "So what happened after I left?"

"Oh, not much. I accepted your help on the job and quickly tied up all the loose ends."

She looked at him suspiciously. Why were his eyes sparkling with so much amusement?

"What do you mean, my help?"

"Well, once you solved the puzzle, it was just a matter of finding the necessary evidence."

"Steve, you have to be one of the most irritating, arrogant, opinionated, self-inflated—"

"What did I say?"

"Nothing! That's the problem. You're acting so damned smug and you're not telling me a thing."

He held up his arms as though attempting to ward off a blow. "All right, all right. I'm just remembering my boss's reaction when I told him what I'd discovered."

"Which was?"

"That Eric Johanson was the head of a large drug smuggling network operating out of Southeast Asia and supplying much of the Australian continent, Africa and Europe. The man we found murdered was an undercover agent posing as a gardener in order to get enough evidence to convict Johanson. What we decided must have happened was that he followed us the day we took our walk, either to see if we were part of the operation or not, and must have seen the sniper who shot at us. It's only conjecture at this point, but your suggestion that he was trying to come to our rescue when he was discovered and killed makes a lot of sense."

"You mean I was right?"

"On the money."

"But you weren't over there checking on Mr. Johanson, were you?"

"The real coincidence in all of this is the fact that the man I was looking for happens to be Johanson's brother."

"Is that why he had us picked up at the airport?"

"Yes. He had been following the news and had seen an excerpt on one of my special reports where I mentioned Trevor Randall's death and the mysterious circumstances surrounding it." He took an appreciative sip of coffee before he went on. "When he found out I was coming to Australia, he felt that my visit was a little too timely with my recent report."

"Then why did he let us go without saying anything?"

"Because he wasn't absolutely convinced there was a connection. He decided not to take a chance, though, and decided to entertain us and keep tabs on us at the same time."

She leaned forward, resting her elbows on the table. "Was he responsible for our being shot at?"

"He denied it and he knows we have no way of proving that he did, but my gut feeling is that he preferred not to take any chances. If we were found, he could always be suitably shocked by the accidental shooting. There would have been a good chance that we might not have been found."

She shuddered. "So you never found anything out about Trevor Randall?"

"I didn't say that."

She straightened. "You mean you found him?"

"Johanson would not tell us his whereabouts. He had reluctantly acknowledged their relationship, but admitted that he had refused to have anything to do with his brother. Luckily my contact there in Sydney was certain that he had seen him, but had trouble placing him, until it hit him. Although Trevor had changed his name, he hadn't bothered to change his appearance. He just found the most unlikely place to hide."

"Where?"

"As a school custodian."

"You mean, a janitor?"

"Well, he had more responsibility than that, but in effect, yes."

"Wasn't he highly educated?"

"Yes, but whatever he had gone through had strongly affected him. I talked to the man at length. He talks of his other life as though it were something he saw on television or at a movie. He has lost touch with reality to the extent that he doesn't realize that he actually lived all the stories he likes to share with his cronies. They think he made them up or read them somewhere. So does he."

"But that's awful."

"I found it rather sad, myself. If he was who we think he was, he spent years in British Intelligence playing an elaborate set of games, with intricate rules, living multiple lives."

"Until he no longer knew who he was."

Steve nodded. "Yes. That's what I think happened. He managed to fake his death and disappear. He even changed his name. After that, he seems to have pretty well fallen apart mentally."

Jessica was quiet for several moments. "You know, that's rather sad, when you think about it."

"I suppose."

"What are you going to do about him?"

"Well, he's certainly no harm to anyone where he is. The stories he tells have no credibility. Any information he might retain has become obsolete."

"So are you going to do a news item on him?"

"I don't think so. It would serve no good purpose at this point. As long as he's still alive, I think he deserves his privacy."

"But you definitely think he was a double agent."

"Yes. He knows too much about how the other side operates. Or how they used to operate."

"He really was a traitor."

"In his mind, he was trying to bring unity to Europe. I guess it's all in your perspective."

"I suppose. We all have to live with our own self-concept."

"Until something so traumatic happens that we're forced to face the discrepancies between who we believe we are and what choices we have to make."

"So when he finally saw himself as a traitor, his mind went."

"That's my guess. He couldn't handle facing that kind of self-knowledge."

Jessica stood and picked up their dishes. While she had her back to him, she said, "So you have to leave tomorrow."

"Yes."

"I'm glad you took the time to come by and tell me what happened. I really appreciate it."

Steve walked over behind her and placed his hands on either side of her waist. "Princess?"

She didn't look around, but continued to vigorously scrub the dishes as though she intended to remove the floral designs off their surfaces. "Yes?"

"We need to talk."

"What have we been doing?"

He slowly turned her until she was facing him. He tilted her head so that she was forced to look up at him.

"I mean about us."

She dropped her gaze, staring at his mouth. "There is no us. You know that."

"Do I?"

She closed her eyes.

"You know that I love you. I've made no effort to hide my feelings for you."

Her eyes had opened at his words. "No," she whispered. "I didn't know."

He shook his head. "And here I was thinking you were so blasted smart. Just shows what I know." He leaned down and placed a gentle kiss on her lips.

"Oh, Steve," she whispered after a moment.

"That's a start," he agreed. "What comes next?"

"I'm scared."

"No, no, no. That is not what comes next. I'm really going to be forced to question your intelligence in a moment. No, you're supposed to say, 'Oh, Steve, I love you, too.'"

"This can't be happening."

"Don't try to fight it, princess. You can't win. This thing is bigger than both of us."

"It will never work. There's too much going against us."

He nibbled on her ear. "Give me thirty reasons why it won't work."

"Thirty!"

He shrugged. "All right. Fifteen."

"Steve, this is serious."

He leaned against her, rubbing his lower body against hers. "I must be training for the Olympics or something. I'll either end up as well conditioned as any athlete or die trying." He gave her another kiss. "But what a way to go."

"We're too different. We fight all the time. Why, we don't even live in the same country."

He gave her another kiss. "That's three. How about twelve more?"

"You're impossible."

"Okay. That's four."

"No, I mean it. I mean, this is ridiculous. How could we explain it to Mom and Michael?"

"Something tells me they already understand about such things. If not, we'll sit down with them and explain in detail, complete with graphs and diagrams."

"Are you ever serious?"

"Only about us."

"But how can there be an us?" she wailed. "My job is here. You're in London."

"What do you bet that if we both put our minds to it, we could probably come up with all kinds of options that would give us innumerable choices."

"I'm scared," Jessica said once again, burying her head in his chest.

"Me, too."

Her head jerked up like a puppet's on a string.

Steve explained. "I'm scared of losing you. It's taken me all these years to get this close to you. What if I go back to London and when I come back you have convinced yourself that you hate me, like you did before?"

"I could never hate you," she whispered, rubbing her cheek against his chest.

He grinned. "That's a good start, anyway." Without warning he picked her up and carried her into the bedroom. He held her above the bed for a moment, then dropped his arms and watched her land with a bounce. He immediately joined her. "I've discovered the secret for perfect domestic tranquility with you, my sweet."

Jessica eyed him uncertainly. "What?"

"Every time you argue with me, I'm going to make love to you, instead."

"Why is it I'm always the one accused of arguing? It takes two to argue, you know."

"I'm only trying to correct your rather warped perspective in an effort to ease your way in life. You just don't appreciate how—"

"Warped perspective! Who do you think you are, anyway? If anyone has a warped perspective, it's got to be you. You seem to see yourself as totally irresistible to women. Well, let me tell you some—*mmphf*."

After several minutes of silence Steve said, "You were saying?"

She just shook her head.

"That's better. Now, as I was saying, I figure that we could plan on a December wedding. If we make it around Christmas, we can have it at the lake. I'm sure the folks would appreciate that, so they won't have to travel with the twins. Then for the honeymoon—"

"You're going too fast. We're not ready. We don't know each other well enough. December is only four months away."

"If you keep arguing with me, I'm going to get the distinct impression that you are doing whatever you can to make sure I'll make love to you . . . Ouch, you bit me."

She smiled.

He rewarded the smile with a kiss. Then another one.

By the time they broke from the third kiss, Steve forgot about teasing her. "You know that I'm right, don't you, princess? We belong together. I know your fears, remember? I will show you that not every man is like your father. Even if every other man is exactly like your father, I'm not. I love you. I would never do anything to betray that love." He held her close for a moment. When he pulled away from her his eyes were suspiciously moist. "I want to be able to live with you forever, love you to distraction, raise a houseful of children that will have a father right there every day until they're grown. Please give us a chance."

"Children?"

"Only if you want them, of course."

"I've never let myself think about them. David and Diane have been the children in my life."

He grinned. "Just think how much they'll enjoy being an aunt and an uncle to our offspring."

"Oh, Steve," Jessica groaned. "I just don't know."

"I do. Believe me, it will work. Trust me enough to know we can do it."

"I can't imagine my life without you in it," she finally admitted.

"I knew it. You see, you were wrong. I am without doubt irresistible."

"Don't let it go to your head."

His laugh reflected his enjoyment of the moment. "Some day you'll thank me for ignoring all your comments and giving you the love you secretly wanted from me."

Jessica touched his cheek, then slowly pulled his mouth down to hers. "Thank you for giving me your love. I'll spend each and every day of my life thanking you, Steve Donovan. Mother was right. You really are Superman."

Their shared laughter rang through the apartment, just as their shared love made the room glow.

Steve knew that they would make it. There was too much love between them not to.

Epilog

What are *you* doing here!" Jessica's shocked surprise did little to hide her joy as she ran across the room and leaped into her husband's arms.

Steve was thankful that he happened to be standing beside their bed when she came out of the bathroom because her momentum caused them both to fall backward onto the bed.

"You sneak," she accused between kisses that she scattered feverishly over his face. "You could have called and warned me. I had no idea you would be back this soon." She pulled back long enough to look at him, then began to kiss him again. "Are you all right? Did the investigation go the way you'd planned?"

Steve started laughing. He couldn't help it. After four years of marriage he would have expected to have grown used to Jessica and her exuberance. The one thing he had learned to expect over the years was that Jessica would always do the unexpected.

She'd been upset when he left. Not that he blamed her. Being called away suddenly on the evening of their Thanksgiving celebration had been tough, particularly at the point where they had been interrupted.

He'd wondered how he was going to handle her when he returned. He'd already planned several tactics that he hoped would help to coax her into a more receptive mood. Obviously he wasn't going to have to use them. This time.

He rolled until he had her on her back beneath him. "May I take it that this means you're glad to see me?" he whispered, nuzzling her neck.

"You wretch. You just caught me off guard. Otherwise I was going to suggest you spend your first evening back with your buddy, Max."

"But he's not nearly so much fun as you are, my love."

His kisses still seemed to have the power to distract her from her pique. Thank God.

"Steve?"

"Mmmmm."

"Are we going to have to cancel our plans to fly back to the States?"

He raised his head and looked at her in surprise. "You mean again?"

Jessica frowned. "That's exactly what I mean. We had to cancel going home for Thanksgiving, but you promised we could be there in time for Christmas and our anniversary."

"No, we're going as scheduled. This case has just dragged on longer than any of us thought it would. This last trip tied up all the loose ends."

She rubbed her cheek against his chest. "I'm so glad you're home. I missed you."

"What did you do with the champagne we were going to have after dinner?"

She smiled. "Saved it, of course. You don't think I would have enjoyed drinking it by myself, do you?"

He took his time and kissed her thoroughly and with obvious longing. When he slowly withdrew his mouth, he whispered, "You know how much I hated leaving you, don't you?"

She nodded, her eyes shining with a hint of moisture.

"You know that I love you very much and would never do anything to intentionally upset you, don't you?"

She nodded again.

"I talked to Max about resigning."

"What did he say?"

"I'm afraid it's not repeatable."

"It's not that I mind, it's just that we can't seem to plan very far ahead."

"But you've enjoyed living in Europe, haven't you?"

"Of course. Who wouldn't enjoy living in all the famous capitals of western Europe, married to a news celebrity like Steven Donovan?"

"Not to mention the fact that you've had some great articles published under your byline over the years."

She grinned. "Free-lance writing is more fun than I thought it would be."

"And you still have your monthly contribution to the travel magazine."

"I know."

"So things aren't all that bad, are they?"

"I'm really not complaining. It's just that I'm a little concerned about the future."

He kissed her once more, unable to resist the temptation of her moist lips so close to his own.

"What's wrong with our future? It looks great."

"For a couple, maybe. But for a family our life-style might be a little too freewheeling."

Steve stopped nibbling on her ear and sat up, staring at her. "Are you saying what I think you're saying?"

Jessica nodded. "That was going to be my big news the night you had to leave. I had it all planned. I'd have my filmy peignoir on as we sat before the fire sipping champagne. Then I'd tell you about the call that had come in earlier in the day from the doctor telling me that—"

"Then it's true! We're finally going to have our family!" Steve started laughing and hugged her tightly for a moment. Then he suddenly let go and stared at her. "I'm sorry. Did I hurt you?" He glanced down at her stomach. "I didn't think about what I was doing."

She hugged him back. "I'm fine. The doctor said everything is exactly as it should be and that we should be increasing the size of our family by midsummer."

"Oh, princess. I'm so proud of you."

She grinned. "I couldn't have done it without you."

"Have you told the folks?"

"Of course not. I haven't told anyone. That's why I was so upset when you got called away so abruptly. All my plans were ruined."

"Not ruined. Just postponed. We can still have the fire, the champagne and your sexy gown."

"Now?"

Since Jessica had walked out of the bathroom wrapped only in a towel, it took very little effort on Steve's part to remove her only article of clothing. It didn't take him much longer to remove his clothing, as well. "The trimming comes later. First things first."

Once again they created the magic that seemed to swirl around them whenever they were together. This time they celebrated their love, their life and their future.

*   *   *   *   *

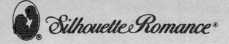

Back by popular demand, some of Diana Palmer's earliest published books are available again!

Several years ago, Diana Palmer began her writing career. Sweet, compelling and totally unforgettable, these are the love stories that enchanted readers everywhere.

Next month, six more of these wonderful stories will be available in DIANA PALMER DUETS—Books 4, 5 and 6. Each DUET contains two powerful stories plus an introduction by Diana Palmer. Don't miss:

Book Four	AFTER THE MUSIC DREAM'S END
Book Five	BOUND BY A PROMISE PASSION FLOWER
Book Six	TO HAVE AND TO HOLD THE COWBOY AND THE LADY

Be sure to look for these titles next month at your favorite retail outlet. If you missed DIANA PALMER DUETS, Books 1, 2 or 3, order them by sending your name, address, zip or postal code, along with a check or money order for $3.25 for each book ordered, plus 75¢ postage and handling, payable to Silhouette Reader Service to:

In the U.S.	In Canada
901 Fuhrmann Blvd.	P.O. Box 609
Box 1396	Fort Erie, Ontario
Buffalo, NY 14269-1396	L2A 5X3

Please specify book title(s) with your order.

DPD-1

Diamond Jubilee Collection

It's our 10th Anniversary...
and *you* get a present!

This collection of early Silhouette
Romances features novels written
by three of your favorite authors:

ANN MAJOR—*Wild Lady*
ANNETTE BROADRICK—*Circumstantial Evidence*
DIXIE BROWNING—*Island on the Hill*

* These Silhouette Romance titles were first published in the early 1980s
  and have not been available since!

* Beautiful Collector's Edition bound in antique green simulated leather to
  last a lifetime!

* Embossed in gold on the cover and spine!

This special collection will not be sold in retail stores and is only available
through this exclusive offer.
Look for details in all Silhouette series published in June, July and August.